RESURRECTION VALLEY

Other books by Danny C. Thornsberry:

Coltrane's Journey

RESURRECTION VALLEY

•

Danny C. Thornsberry

AVALON BOOKS
NEW YORK

PRINTED IN THE UNITED STATES OF AMERICA
ON ACID-FREE PAPER
BY HADDON CRAFTSMEN, BLOOMSBURG, PENNSYLVANIA

For my parents, Harve and Rachel Thornsberry.

CONTENTS

Chapter 1:   THE WAGONS ROLL   1

Chapter 2:   LEANER AND MEANER   13

Chapter 3:   A SIMPLE PLEASURE   22

Chapter 4:   JOINING UP   31

Chapter 5:   LEANTOWN   38

Chapter 6:   PROSPERITY   51

Chapter 7:   COLE JACKSON   65

Chapter 8:   LAW AND ORDER   83

Chapter 9:   TRAIL HAND   98

Chapter 10: THE EXPEDITION   113

Chapter 11: THE REUNION   131

Chapter 12: HOMECOMING   146

Chapter 13: POLITICS   157

Chapter 14: THE RECKONING   175

Chapter One
The Wagons Roll

S tanding at just over six feet tall, the thirty-year-old Ethan Jackson had been described as a man who was broad of shoulder and strong of back. And the .45 Colt he wore on his hip wasn't just there for show. He could use it now, and had used it before, with lethal results.

Having held more than one job in his life requiring a familiarity with firearms, he had developed quite a skill with that short-gun. As a matter of fact, if pressed, Ethan would have to admit that almost all of the jobs he had held during his life required the skilled use of a weapon at one time or another.

Sometimes it seemed that he just couldn't keep from gravitating toward violence. It was similar to the way an old fire horse ran toward the smell of smoke, the only difference being that the smoke Ethan ran toward was gun smoke. And whenever he smelled that odor he had to be in on the action.

At least that was the way it had been. But all of the years he spent living the brutal life of a cowhand and the time spent wearing a tin star in too many wild cow towns had taken a toll. And now Ethan was looking for a more peaceful way of making a living.

He would have preferred settling in one of the towns where he made his living wearing a badge, but he had developed a reputation as a man who was fast with a gun. And there was always some fool kid riding into whatever town Ethan happened to be working in wanting to be known as the man who put Ethan Jackson in his grave. Even when he wore a badge there was always somebody waiting for him in the street willing to risk having the law after him for gunning down a duly appointed lawman just in hopes of getting a reputation, a reputation Jackson would have given anything to be shut of. That was why he was in Missouri joining a wagon train bound for Oregon. He hoped by moving to that far territory his reputation could be left behind.

Ethan was eager to get to where he could start living his new life, and he would have preferred to make tracks for Oregon traveling light and fast on the back of the roan stallion tied to the tailgate of the Conestoga wagon he was driving. But he was loaded down with all types of tools and foodstuffs needed to start a homestead. So the journey would be long and slow.

While Ethan had chosen to live a quieter life, he hadn't given up the simple pleasures of life. He had no intention of traveling over hundreds of miles of new country and not doing some sight-seeing, hunting, fishing, and, like most men of the time, hunting for the yellow metal that set fire to men's souls.

With that in mind, Ethan had hired a driver for his wagon who went by the name of Jake Collins, a grizzled old man who appeared to be pushing sixty and who claimed to have done everything in the West worth doing.

Ethan couldn't vouch for Jake's claim that he could do

everything that there was to do on the frontier, but he could swear on a stack of Bibles, as high as anyone would care to pile them, that Collins knew his way around a cook fire. Ethan would have been hard pressed to remember a time when he had sat down to grub as tasty as Jake could put together.

Collins claimed to have learned his craft from years living in Mexico and among the different Indian tribes when he had been a mountain man running a trapline in the Rockies. But of the two peoples, Jake gave the Mexicans credit for teaching him how to put the flavor in his food. He gave the Indians credit for teaching him about healing roots and the proper way to scalp and torture a man.

Jackson hoped that Collins was kidding about the scalping and torturing parts but, all things considered, Ethan figured he had ended up with a teamster, cook, and doctor at the bargain price of forty a month.

Awakened by a jolt from the wagon wheel hitting a rut in the road, Collins, who had been sleeping off last night's celebration in the back of the wagon, raised himself up on one elbow and said, "You know it'd be a good idea if'n at least one of us stayed awake while the durn wagon was movin'. 'Specially the one holdin' the reins. That way he'd see the chuck holes 'afore he ran into 'em. And it'd make things a lot easier for those of us who ain't as young and spry as we used to be."

Fishing among the supplies in the back of the wagon, Jake took out a bottle of what Ethan assumed was a remedy for a hangover and joined him on the front seat. "Want me to take the reins for awhile, Ethan?" he asked.

"No need, sun's just about overhead, we'll be noonin' in a few minutes."

"I doubt that muddle-headed wagonmaster knows that when the sun is directly over his head that it's noontime. I swear sometimes I think that old boy has wood chips for brains," Jake said.

Anybody who didn't know that Jake and the wagon master, Tom Johnson, were old friends going back to their days of hunting buffalo together on the plains would have thought that Collins really had a grudge against the fifty-year-old man who organized the trip to Oregon. But Ethan knew that it was only good-natured joshing that Jake was engaging in.

"You're just grumpy from the hangover and you want to take it out on old Tom," Ethan said, slapping the reins on the backs of the four horses pulling the heavy wagon.

Smiling, Jake pulled out a plug of black tobacco and bit off a large chunk of it. Working it around in his mouth a bit, he took aim at a bug crawling alongside the road and nailed it at twenty feet with some of the amber juice.

Satisfied that he still had the "touch," he turned to Ethan and said, "You never did say what you was plannin' on doin' when you got to Oregon, Ethan, and if'n it ain't no big secret or nothin', I'm an old man with an old woman's curiosity who's been wonderin' about what you got on your mind to do when we get there."

Ethan looked thoughtful as he answered. "It's no secret. I haven't talked about what my plans are 'cause I don't have any, other than taking up some land and building a cabin on it. After that, I suppose I'll take a stab at farming or trapping. I might even decide on taking up the hunt for gold again. I've had a good bit of experience at that already. I suppose if I'd been more inclined to live the life of a hermit, that's what I'd of done with my life."

Looking at Ethan out of the corner of his eye, Collins asked, "You figurin' on keepin' that hogleg you got strapped on in its holster all the way to Oregon, son?"

Ethan hadn't told Jake about his reputation, but the fact

that he knew about it didn't surprise him. The name of Ethan Jackson was well known among people on the frontier, and he'd no doubt that several people on the wagon train knew who he was but had been too polite to mention it.

Tightening his grip on the reins, Ethan said, "I hope I can, for if there's one thing I'd like to leave behind, it's my reputation as a gunman."

Working up some more tobacco juice, Collins let fly with another stream of the liquid toward the road. "I wish you luck, son, but people bein' the way they are, and the times bein' as rough as they is, I doubt that pistol'll stay in its holster for very long. And if you're lookin' for some place where your reputation as a gun hand won't follow you, all I can say is that you'd better think some more about becoming a hermit, for that's the only way—other than gettin' beat to the draw—you're going to lose that reputation."

Ethan couldn't disagree with what Jake had said. Although he would have liked to believe he could spend the rest of his life without ever having to fire his gun in anger, he already knew the world was filled with people who were willing to kill a man for something as stupid as gaining a reputation as a gunslinger, or in some places, for as little as the clothes on his back.

With his mind occupied, Ethan failed to see the chuckhole as the wagon wheel rolled in and bounced out of it, jarring his bones and eliciting a groan from Collins. Sore and tired, Jackson was ready for a rest when Johnson called a halt a few minutes later.

Ethan hadn't had much of a chance to get to know any of the people traveling in the twenty other wagons of the train. Mostly he only knew something about the people in the wagon in front and the folks who were bringing up the tail end of the train directly behind him.

The people in the wagon in front of his were named Baldwin—John and Mary and their two children, Josh, age ten, and Lucy, age eight. Jake had told him that John Baldwin had been a schoolteacher back in Ohio and was headed for Oregon to start a farm. Eventually, as more settlers arrived, he hoped to open up a school. Ethan figured him to be a good prospect for a neighbor and was happy to be traveling with him.

On the other hand, the folks traveling behind him at the very end of the train were a different matter altogether. There were two of them named Leary. A man in his early thirties who went by the name of Lonnie and his much-put-upon wife named Alice.

What Ethan disliked most about Lonnie was the way he failed to keep his wagon in shape. He couldn't seem to remember to grease his wagon's axle, but always kept himself well lubricated with corn whiskey.

Jackson knew the Learys to be the weak link in the chain that held the wagon train together, and so did the wagon boss who put their wagon at the end of the line where they wouldn't slow down the rest of the group.

From the shape their wagon was in, Ethan figured them to end up with more than their fair share of breakdowns. Johnson had originally denied them permission to join the group, but Alice Leary had pleaded with him to let them join, saying they had nowhere else to go.

Ethan had sympathy for the woman, but realizing what a liability the Learys would be on the trail, he wished that Johnson had hardened his heart and refused to let them join the wagon train. He felt that letting someone so poorly prepared come along on what was going to be a journey over country filled with renegades, wild animals, and natural hazards would be much crueler than just telling them no to begin with.

The wagons had been on the trail for two weeks and were averaging about fifteen miles each day with everything going along without a hitch. The road had been level and dry, allowing the people to fall into a routine. Meals were prepared three times a day with the members of four or five wagons getting together to pool their resources at each stop. With each group sharing a campfire, most of them rotated cooking duties, each member taking a turn.

The group Jackson belonged to consisted of the Baldwins, the Learys, and a large family from the hills of Eastern Kentucky named Kenton. The head of the clan was named Caleb and, along with his wife, Martha, he rode herd over a brood of seven children who ranged in age from sixteen to five years old.

While the other groups rotated the cooking chores, Jake had pretty much staked out his claim as the chief cook among his group. And while this made extra work for him, he had no shortage of helpers when it came to the women of the group. Not only because of the fairness of the situation, but because they wanted to learn Collins's way of cooking.

Ethan figured that the only fly in the ointment was the Learys. Really, the only problem was Lonnie Leary. His wife was helpful and inoffensive, but Lonnie was neither helpful nor easy to get along with.

Not only had the predicted breakdowns of the Leary wagon occurred with great regularity, but Lonnie had proven worthless when it came to helping anyone else on the wagon train. Of course, with all of his problems with his own gear, no one expected him to be of much help to anyone else, and with plenty of willing hands to help out, nobody much cared that he was a lazy lout. What really galled most everyone, however, were Leary's overbearing ways.

Being a big man, larger than everyone else on the train, he was quick to try and force everyone else to bend to his wishes. But he hadn't been successful at bullying the group Jackson belonged to. At least not so far. For while he was taller and heavier than everyone in the group, he knew that his size was no match for Ethan's Colt, or the squirrel rifle Kenton carried like it was an extension of his arm. Even old Collins carried a razor-sharp skinning knife at his side that he could have used to carve the big man up with as skillfully as he did a side of beef.

That left only the schoolteacher, John Baldwin, for him to harass, and on that night of the second week out of St. Louis, Lonnie was in his cups even more than usual. Frustrated from a day of wagon breakdowns, he was looking for a dog to kick, and he was looking at Baldwin like his first name was Rover.

"Think you're better than the rest of us, don't you, schoolteacher?" taunted Lonnie, as John filled his plate from the large kettle over the fire.

Having experienced Leary's tactics before, John knew the easiest way to weather the storm was to ignore him and move to a corner where he would be out of sight of the brute. Before long, Lonnie's limited attention span and the whiskey would reduce him to a bumbling idiot who would have to be helped to his own wagon.

But that night was different. When John moved away, Lonnie got to his feet and followed him.

"What's the matter, schoolteacher? I asked you a question and you're going to answer it or I'm going to wring your scrawny little neck," Leary said, reaching for Baldwin's throat.

"Sit down, Leary," ordered Jackson.

Turning to his right, Lonnie faced Ethan and loosed his rage on the ex-lawman. "Well, if it ain't the killer. What about it, killer, you able to face a man without that gun in your hand?" Leary asked. His inner voice was warning him to shut up, but it couldn't break through the whiskey-induced fog to his besotted brain, and since a gun hadn't been pulled on him yet, he became even bolder in his taunts. "I didn't think so. You're just like all those other big-shot gunfighters—you carry your manhood in your holster." Leary was smirking and didn't see the blow coming. A powerful backhand from Ethan made him stagger backwards until he fell on his butt.

Wiping his bleeding mouth, Lonnie looked up to see Ethan unbuckle and hand his holstered weapon over to Baldwin. Rolling up his sleeves, Jackson said, "All right Leary, you been riding roughshod over a lot of people lately. I reckon it's about time to show you the error of your ways."

Smiling, Leary got to his feet. Lonnie knew that Jackson was unaware of how vicious he could be and the power he could put behind his ham-like hands when he balled them into fists and started throwing punches. So, as he walked toward Ethan, who had moved to the center of the camp, he was brimming with confidence. He was going to show that ex-lawman what pain was all about. Well, at least he would experience what pain was like while he remained alive. The way Leary figured it, Jackson could have spent his last day on earth. He wouldn't be the first man he had killed with his fists. It all depended on how long the men in camp let the fight go on before they pulled him off Jackson. At the very least, he was counting on breaking some of Ethan's bones.

Ethan Jackson was a big man, but he was dwarfed by the bulk of Leary as he approached him in the center of the ring formed by the curious onlookers.

Smiling and confident, Lonnie walked up to Ethan and

threw a vicious roundhouse punch at his head with the intent of delivering a killing blow. Halfway through the swing, he closed his eyes in anticipation of the jarring effect Jackson's skull would have on his knuckles.

The momentum of the swing pulled the big man off balance when his fist failed to make contact with its intended target, giving Ethan the opportunity to deliver a hard left cross to Lonnie's right temple and, just before backpedaling out of range, two quick jabs to his opponent's ribs.

The blows delivered had been powerful but Leary soaked up the punishment and lunged for Ethan once again. When he got within range, he threw another punch.

Weaving and ducking, Ethan slipped under the blow with Leary's fist grazing his right shoulder, and as he came up he delivered a left uppercut that snapped Lonnie's head back. He then danced quickly out of reach.

Lonnie had planned on overwhelming Ethan quickly with brute force and then killing or crippling him at his leisure. What was happening now was completely unexpected. He was used to standing toe to toe and slugging it out. He had no idea how to fight somebody like Jackson who danced and darted all over the place like some sort of a hummingbird.

Plus, the blows he had been receiving had started to take effect—his strength was starting to seep away. So when Ethan shot a straight punch to his face, Lonnie was stunned to the point where he didn't even see the blows that brought him to his knees or the roundhouse that put him to sleep.

No bones had been broken, but anyone who looked at Leary's face over the next two weeks would be able to see that he had been in a rough-and-tumble fight and come out on the short end of the dispute.

Returning to his own campfire, Ethan found a wagon tongue to rest on and watched several men carry Lonnie past him to his own wagon where his wife could tend to his bruises.

Watching the men who had carried Lonnie return, Ethan noticed that the crowd hadn't dispersed, and that they were all milling about and talking to the wagon master. Apparently there was some sort of an argument going on and all attention was centering on Tom Johnson.

Ethan figured that the people in the crowd were complaining about Lonnie Leary since he'd been bullying several members of the train and they no doubt wanted him gone. And from the way Johnson was holding up his hands it was obvious that he was trying to calm the crowd.

Then he saw Jake and Baldwin join Tom in trying to calm the complaining mob. He couldn't figure why those two would take up the fight to keep the Learys with the group, and he was too far away from the crowd to hear what was being said.

If he hadn't been so tired, Ethan would have walked over to find out what was happening. It appeared that someone was calling for a vote, with one man jumping atop a wagon wheel and yelling out, "All in favor of throwing him off the train, say aye!"

A loud chorus of male voices said, "Aye!"

"Opposed?"

"Nay!" came the reply from Jake and Baldwin.

"The ayes have it," said the man atop the wagon wheel. "He leaves in the morning."

Cheers erupted from the crowd, and everyone returned to his own camp.

Ethan was standing when Tom Johnson walked up to him.

"You hear all that commotion, Ethan?" asked Johnson.

"Yep. What was it all about, Tom?"

Turning his hat brim in his hands and looking uncomfortable, Johnson said, "According to the bylaws drawn up in St. Louis, a majority of the folks traveling on this train can vote someone off of it at any time."

"I remember," Ethan said. "I was there when the articles were drawn up."

"Well," said Johnson, "they had a vote and you just been kicked off the train."

Chapter Two
Leaner and Meaner

Ethan had been surprised by his ouster from the wagon train. He'd been unaware of the hostility that many of the people held for him. None of them knew him personally, but they all knew of his reputation as a killer. Of course, all of those he killed had been outlaws who were trying to kill him at the time. But that didn't matter to those who voted him off the train. He was a killer and that was that. It didn't make any difference that if he had been a bounty hunter instead of a man wearing a badge he would have gotten rich collecting the rewards posted on the heads of the men he shot in the line of duty. Instead, he ended up being hated and feared by a bunch of eastern greenhorns who had no idea about what life was like in the West and what a man sometimes had to do to survive.

But the greenhorns were in the majority and their decision had to be honored. It didn't matter how stupid and prejudiced the decision was, Ethan had to abide by it as he sat astride his horse that morning watching the wagons roll westward. Yesterday there had been twenty-one wagons making up the train, but on that morning there were only eighteen. When Baldwin and Kenton found out that Jackson was continuing on by himself, they asked to join him. At first Ethan warned them that three wagons made a much more appealing target to renegades than a wagon train the size of Johnson's and they would be safer staying with the wagon boss. But Baldwin said he and his wife were willing to take their chances with him and at the very least they would be free of Lonnie Leary.

As for Caleb Kenton, he was just plain mad. He'd been on a hunt and was late getting back to camp the night of the altercation and impromptu meeting that resulted in Jackson being ousted by the so-called good citizens of the train. When his wife told him about what had happened he became enraged and stomped off to find Johnson to express his opinion on the matter.

On his way to find the wagon boss he had run into Jim Cooper, the man who owned the wagon traveling in front of the Kentons. Taking Caleb aside, Jim had started bragging about how he'd been one of the men who'd called for a vote to rid the train of the ex-lawman. Caleb could tell that Cooper expected him to congratulate him for doing his civic duty. Caleb expressed his gratitude by throwing a right cross that landed on Cooper's chin and knocked him flat on his back. Stepping over the body, Kenton had continued his search for Johnson.

Later that night, Cooper had circulated among his friends trying to get up another vote to throw the man he referred to as "that blasted hotheaded hillbilly" off the train.

His efforts had been a waste of time on two counts. First, since everyone who knew the little man was aware of how foolishly he ran his mouth, many of them had felt like doing what Kenton had done on more than one occasion themselves. Secondly, Caleb Kenton quit the train himself that night, saying he wanted nothing to do with a bunch of people who could vote off a man like Ethan Jackson who had faced up to Lonnie Leary and, without resorting to his gun, kicked the big man's overbearing butt.

So a new wagon train was formed, with Jake Collins, the most experienced of the group, acting as wagon boss. He hadn't sought the position and only agreed to take it when he discovered that the job would mostly involve acting as a guide. All of the major decisions would be made by a committee made up of Kenton, Baldwin, and Jackson.

The first decision of the new committee was to make a side trip to a nearby town to restock their stores and to better arm John Baldwin and train him in the proper use of a rifle and a handgun.

After returning from town, Ethan took Baldwin aside to give him some instructions on how to use his new weapons.

The only firearm the ex-schoolteacher had ever owned was an ancient double-barreled twelve-gauge shotgun. An effective weapon at close range, but at any distance over forty yards it was pretty much useless. It was also heavy and unwieldy, making it likely John wouldn't have it with him when he needed it most. That was the reason Jackson recommended John buy one of the newer model Colt revolvers in .45 caliber with a three inch-barrel that had come to be known as the "store-keeper's" model due to its lighter weight and compactness, which made it easier to conceal. When worn in a holster designed for inside the waistband of a pair of pants, it proved to be very comfortable.

After warning Baldwin to make sure to let the firing pin rest on an empty chamber for safety, Ethan took him away from camp for a bit of target practice.

Picking up an empty paint can he had brought from town, Ethan walked fifty feet away and set it on the ground. Walking back to Baldwin, he pointed at the can and said, "Try it."

Taking careful aim with the Colt, John pulled the trigger. A cloud of dust appeared two feet to the right of the paint can.

"You're flinching," Jackson said.

"What's that?" Baldwin asked.

Taking the weapon from the new pistolero, Ethan turned his back to Baldwin for a few seconds and when he turned back he handed the revolver to the former schoolteacher and said, "Try it now."

Lining up the front sight of the pistol on the can once again, Baldwin pulled the trigger. This time, instead of a hollow boom, there was a click. When he opened his eyes, John could see that the gun's barrel was pointing to the right.

"You closed your eyes and you jerked the gun to the right when you pulled the trigger," Jackson said as he walked up and asked John for the gun. Taking the pistol, he opened up the loading gate and showed Baldwin the gun was empty.

"I took the bullets out so you could see what you were doing wrong. What I want you to do now is to line up the sight like the gun was loaded and squeeze the trigger. When you move your finger, try not to move the rest of your hand."

Doing as he was told, John noticed that he was still pulling the barrel to the right when the hammer dropped on an empty chamber, but by the fifth try the sight was holding steadily on the can when the trigger was pulled.

"Want to try it again?" asked Jackson.

Taking the offered weapon, Ethan opened the loading gate and put in one cartridge. Spinning the cylinder, he handed the pistol back to Baldwin, saying, "You have one bullet. Pull the trigger six times and I guarantee it will go off sooner or later. You just won't know when it's going to happen. That way you'll be able to tell if you're still flinching when you pull the trigger."

Once again, Baldwin lined up the sight and squeezed the trigger. There was the sound of a click, and he eared the hammer back to full-cock again. This time, when he squeezed the trigger, there was an explosion and the gun bucked in his hand. The paint can he'd been aiming at flew into the air.

A bit more practice and Baldwin was hitting his target almost every time. Since he had some experience firing a rifle before, Baldwin spent much less time familiarizing himself with the Winchester model '73 in .44–.40 caliber. In the end, Baldwin was as well equipped in the firearms line as any man on the Oregon trail.

Ethan's party spent the rest of the day mending harnesses and clothes and writing letters to the folks back home. Collins planned to start on the trail the next morning and stay behind Johnson's outfit all the way to Oregon. At least that was the plan. But Jake figured that a wagon train made up of a bunch of greenhorns who had the tendency not to follow the advice of an experienced wagon boss like Tom Johnson were destined to have their wagons come to a grinding halt sooner or later. And he would be forced to steer around them. He didn't know how long it would take to happen, but he had no doubt that it would.

That night around the campfire there was some speculation about who the Learys would be taking their meals with and how long it would take for Lonnie to act up again. Kenton said that it would probably be Jim Cooper's group, since with the absence of Jackson, Baldwin, and himself, Cooper would be the next in line to be followed by Lonnie's wagon. Remembering that he had slugged the loudmouth the night before, Caleb allowed as to how he hoped that would be the case. Especially after he found out it had been Cooper who had jumped atop a wagon wheel and called for the vote that resulted in Ethan being thrown off the train.

The next morning the people and animals were well rested from the day's break from traveling and eager to be on their way. Collins appeared to be particularly feisty. Ethan kidded him that it was because of the weight of his new office as wagon master.

The animals, wagons, and people were all in excellent shape and Collins would prove to be a first-rate wagon boss. As guide he proved to know the best sections of the trail to use to move the fastest and with the least effort. As a result of all these advantages, their group of three wagons soon caught sight of Johnson.

This presented a problem. They couldn't join the wagons in Tom Johnson's outfit, and they didn't want to eat their dust for endless miles down the trail. So it was decided as soon as the wagons in the train ahead of them nooned, they would continue on and pass them by.

The first wagon they passed as they continued on their way that afternoon was Lonnie Leary's. Several men were gathered around it in hopes of patching it up so that it would continue to roll until night camp. It was a familiar sight that Ethan had good cause to remember, since his former position on the train had meant that he was always the first one on the scene when the incompetent Leary needed help.

Jackson could see that Lonnie had recovered enough to be up and watching other men doing a job that should have been his. He glared at Jackson as he passed by, but Ethan only smiled and tipped his hat to the dour and spiteful man as he urged his horses forward.

Baldwin's wagon was in the middle of the Collins's train and when Lonnie saw him he lumbered forward and grabbed John's horse's reins, halting the team. Walking stiffly over to John, he climbed up on the driver's seat and grabbed him by the throat as he had done the night before. He started to tell Baldwin that his time had come, but froze when he heard the metallic click of a hammer being eared back and felt the cold barrel of John's Colt pressed under his chin.

Seeing the look of death in the former schoolteacher's eyes, Leary quickly released his grip on the man's throat like it was a rattlesnake he'd accidentally picked up.

Dropping back down to the ground, Lonnie started backing away toward his crippled wagon, but he was stopped by Baldwin's voice.

"Leary, the next time you try to lay your hands on me, I pull the trigger," he said, letting the hammer down on the pistol and dropping it back into the holster in his waistband.

Turning around, Lonnie hurried back to his wagon, well aware that Baldwin meant what he said. He had seen it in his eyes when he held the gun under his chin. He'd been lucky John hadn't dropped the hammer on him then.

When Kenton, who was bringing up the rear, passed by him, Leary turned his back to him to show his disdain for the Kentuckian. But if truth be told, Lonnie was more than a little unnerved about what had just happened with Baldwin, and he was afraid that the man from the hills lacked the restraint of the former schoolteacher and might just put a ball between his eyes from the squirrel rifle he carried.

They soon passed their former traveling companions and had traveled about a quarter mile when Tom Johnson rode up to Jackson's wagon.

Pushing back his hat, he faced Ethan and said, "Sorry about the vote and all, Ethan. They're all a bunch of dang fools and I told 'em so. But there ain't nothin' I can do about it."

Jackson knew he was telling the truth. Johnson was a Western man who knew how things stood out in the wild country. But he was like a lot of the old mountain men who, when the bottom fell out of the fur market, had to find a way to make a living. Many of them took jobs as guides leading settlers to their new homes. Some became guides for dudes who were out for a bit of sport, hunting game in the Wild West.

Either way they lost what they prized the most—the freedom to do as they pleased. And many times, for the sake of a steady job, they had to swallow their pride and indulge the whims of the greenhorns they worked for.

"I know, Tom. The people you work for don't understand how things work out here, but they'll learn," said Jackson, in an effort to ease Johnson's discomfort at apologizing for the stupidity of the people he was in charge of.

"If the idiots live long enough to learn," added Collins.

Smiling, Johnson said, "Amen to that, Jake."

Turning his horse, Tom tipped his hat to Ethan and rode back to his wagons.

Looking over at Collins, Jackson asked, "What about it, Jake? You think I'm crazy trying to make a go of it with just three wagons?"

Sending a stream of tobacco juice at a bee buzzing by, Jake wiped his mouth with his sleeve and said, "I had me an uncle one time who lived to be ninety-five years old, and once he got past eighty, he started losing weight. Every year he just got to be skinnier and skinnier. One day I asked his boy 'bout how long he figured his pa could hang on a droppin' weight like he was. But his son told me not to pay any attention to him a losin' the pounds. He claimed that his pa aged the same way an old razor-backed hog did. Every year he just gets leaner and meaner. The way I figure it, those other wagons weren't nothin' but extra weight.

And fat's only useful if you plan on hibernatin'. If'n you're plannin' on doin' some travelin', extra weight only slows you down. The way I see it we just been trimmed down to where we're leaner and meaner—the same as my old uncle."

Snapping the reins, Ethan said, "I hope you're right."

Chapter Three
A Simple Pleasure

It had been eight weeks since Jackson's people had split with Tom Johnson's group, and with Ethan's wagons rapidly outpacing the wagon train saddled with Lonnie Leary, they were now a week ahead of Johnson and within sight of Fort Laramie in the Wyoming territory—two days south of the Big Horn Mountains. The night before, the committee Jackson belonged to had a meeting where it was decided they would spend a few days at Fort Laramie where they could make some much-needed repairs and give the people and their animals a chance to rest.

Almost everyone decided to take advantage of the break to rest, but Ethan was determined to ride for the Big Horn Mountains and do some prospecting.

It was the middle of summer—the best time of the year to look for gold in the mountains. Actually, it was the only time anyone could hunt for gold at the higher elevations, for while the water was still ice cold during the summer, at least it was still water that hadn't frozen to ice.

Feeling rested and relaxed after breathing the clean crisp air of the mountains instead of the gritty trail dust he was accustomed to, Ethan rode into a wide flat area between two peaks. Following a creek that ran parallel to both of them, he saw a branch of the creek that looked promising and turned the roan up the shallow pebble-strewn stream in search of a likely spot to search for the yellow metal.

Ethan was soon disappointed when he discovered the banks of the stream to be so close together and the water flowing from such a high elevation that even a metal as heavy as gold wouldn't be able to settle on the stream bed when flooding occurred. So he moved from the open field to a narrow stretch of ground and disappeared between two hills well peppered with aspen and pines.

Eventually he came upon several large boulders strewn in and around a meandering stream. Ethan's attention became fixed on one large stone in particular when a trout chasing a nymph broke the surface of a pool of water and made a splash that startled his horse and focused his attention there.

The location of the boulder made it a natural trap for any gold traveling downstream. Ethan had worked long enough with a gold pan to know that if there was any gold in that stream it would have to be under that rock. And if there was any gold there—there would be a lot of it.

Jackson carried a small pry bar in his saddlebags for just such occasions as this, but he knew that a job of this size would require much more leverage than could be provided by such a small tool. Figuring the pay-off would be well worth the trouble, Ethan dismounted and hobbled his horse.

Digging deep into his saddlebag, Jackson fished out a hatchet and walked a short distance up the branch. Finding a hickory sapling of about four feet in length with a two inch diameter, he cut it down and dragged it back to the large rock. Wedging one end of the tree under the boulder, he placed some flat rocks under the pole and a couple of feet back to provide a spot on which to pivot. Then he waded to the other end of the lever where he put all his weight on the pole in an attempt to dislodge the heavy stone. On Ethan's third attempt, the pole snapped in two, causing him to fall into the icy water.

Not being one to give up, Ethan cut another pole—this one thicker and longer—and resumed his efforts to move the heavy stone. It took several attempts, but he finally forced the large rock to topple over into the pool, sending up a spray that once again covered him from head to toe in icy water. Ignoring his discomfort, Jackson ran to where the boulder had been and peered into the muddy water that was slowly clearing. Seeing light reflecting off of something at the bottom of the stream, he continued to stare into the murky water until he spotted a huge gold nugget.

Ethan spent the rest of the day digging and panning under the circular area the stone had been covering until he hit bedrock. When he finally finished his work he'd recovered every nugget, flake, and bit of dust that had been hiding under that rock for the last hundred years.

The best he could figure, Ethan estimated that that one "pocket" had netted him over $500 worth of gold. And with more time and better equipment, he figured he could dig out a fortune from under those boulders scattered in and around the creek. What he really wanted to do, though, was to explore farther up the stream in hopes of finding where the gold started before it ended up trapped beneath those large rocks worn smooth and lost most of its weight from its long trip down the meandering creek.

The Big Horn Mountains were in an isolated part of the territory where a man was more likely to meet up with a hostile Sioux or Cheyenne—not to mention the occasional grizzly—instead of another miner. It was a dangerous country for a man to be traveling in alone. What was needed to properly explore and mine the area was a well-equipped and well-armed expedition.

Since he lacked the time and the proper equipment to do a good job exploring and mining the region, Ethan figured his best bet was to ride for Fort Laramie at first light and make plans to return to the mountains when he could put together such an expedition.

But for the moment, Jackson was experiencing a cold chill down his spine that wasn't caused by his earlier dip in the icy water, and for some reason he felt an overpowering urge to get out of the mountains. But common sense told him that it was smarter to wait for morning than to try to travel at night. With that in mind, he collected some dry wood and set to building a small cook fire in a spot well hidden from prying eyes.

Taking advantage of the last dying rays of sunlight, Ethan took out a length of fishing line to which he attached a hook baited with a strip of jerky and cast it into the pool where he'd spotted the trout earlier. It wasn't long before he dragged a heavy brown trout to shore and set to roasting it over the fire. That night he ate his supper under the stars and made plans to return to the place he had begun to think of as "Boulder Branch."

It was cold the next morning as he rode down the mountain carrying three bulging leather sacks stuffed with over two pounds of raw gold. He figured Fort Laramie could be reached within two days if he rode the stallion hard, but while he dearly wanted to let the horse run, he held it back, for on one of the many occasions he'd turned back to fix some landmark in his mind, he had spotted the movement of an Indian ducking behind a tree.

He was being followed. He figured it was probably the Sioux who were behind him. He now understood the urge he had felt to get out of the mountains. He was well aware that more than one man had lost his scalp in the mountains for no other reason than the fact he happened to be handy and the warrior carried a knife and a grudge.

Even if the Indian had a reason to hate the white man, Jackson himself hadn't done anything to the red man, and now that he had an opportunity to get rich—he preferred to live.

Ethan had no intention of letting his hair end up on some brave's lance or decorating a warrior's lodge pole. So he rode wary in the saddle with his eyes scanning every tree and rock capable of hiding an enemy, his hand never far from the pistol at his side.

It was common knowlege that trouble was brewing between the tribes and the U.S. Army, and with someone like Colonel George Armstrong Custer—a man with strong political aspirations—pushing for a fight so he could cover himself with glory, it was only a matter of time before the territory erupted into open warfare.

Ethan didn't want any trouble, but he knew that merely riding through country claimed by the Sioux was enough to get a white man killed. The way he saw things, he was only one man riding alone. And armed with only a Colt revolver and a Winchester rifle he was no threat to any of the tribes. If some Indian decided to kill him it could only be called one thing—murder!

If Red Cloud and Sitting Bull were spoiling for a fight, Ethan hoped they'd take it up with the long-haired colonel and leave him alone. All Jackson wanted was to be left alone so he could try to get rich digging in the dirt of the Wyoming territory. And to Jackson's way of thinking, that kind of greed was preferable to getting a lot of men killed to further one's political career. Jackson considered himself a lucky man that he was a civilian and not in the Seventh Cavalry.

The farther down the mountain Ethan rode the higher the little hairs on the back of his neck stood up. Even as he moved to the lower elevations where the air became noticeably warmer he still felt an unnerving chill; especially after he spotted the smoke signals behind him.

The stallion beneath Ethan could feel the ex-lawman tense and it began fidgeting, eager to take the bit in its mouth and get on down the trail. Jackson was also eager to run, and was not only having a hard time keeping his horse under control, but himself as well. The ground he was riding over was strewn with small rocks and pebbles though that made riding over it like trying to walk over marbles. If he tried to run his horse over such terrain, there was a good chance the roan would stumble and fall. If his horse went down—it was over.

Soon, however he was riding on more stable ground. He was just getting ready to let the stallion take the bit in his mouth and run full-out for Fort Laramie when he spotted movement in a stand of aspen to his left. Concentrating, he made out the form of a warrior just as he released his bowstring, sending an arrow toward Jackson's head.

Ethan felt the wind from the feathered shaft as it passed within half an inch of his left earlobe.

Kicking the roan in its ribs, Ethan leaned forward and urged the stallion into a gallop—the time for caution had passed. His only chance was to outrun his attackers and he planned to give them a run for their money when it came to giving up his scalp.

For several minutes Ethan rode at a dangerous pace, dodging trees and boulders and clearing ditches so wide that most horses wouldn't even have attempted to jump them. The roan finally was brought up short by a pile of brush placed in the trail to block Jackson's escape.

Running from behind the brush pile, an Indian began to

wave a brightly colored blanket in an attempt to spook Ethan's horse into throwing him off. While Ethan made a valiant attempt to remain in the saddle, it would have taken a miracle for him to stay aboard that wildly thrashing bronc. During one of the animal's attempts at imitating a fighting fish on a line, Jackson was thrown into a tree which stunned the former sheriff and left him helpless.

Temporarily addled, Ethan could have easily been killed if the brave hadn't been so preoccupied with trying to avoid the crazed stallion's slashing hooves.

The Sioux brave's intention had been to merely spook the horse, not turn it into a crazed beast. So while the warrior really wanted to go after the white man and finish him off, he was forced instead to take refuge behind the brush until the enraged animal had vented its fury and bolted back up the trail.

The roan's attack bought Ethan enough time to get to his feet where he dodged the knife thrust at his belly by the warrior who came from behind the brush and lunged for him. Twisting to the left and using his hip, Jackson threw his attacker to the ground.

While his quick action had turned aside the attack, Ethan had failed to disarm his opponent—a fact he soon became aware of when he began to feel the warm blood flowing down his cheek. The red man had cut him, while being thrown to the ground, reaching out with the blade to slash Jackson across his face.

Backing up, Ethan's right hand went for the Colt at his side—but the holster was empty. He'd been riding with the thong off the hammer due to his feeling of unease and the weapon had fallen out somewhere on the trail during his wild ride.

Bringing up an empty right hand, Jackson blocked the

Sioux's knife and, with a hard right hook, smashed the brave's left temple causing the Indian to drop his weapon.

A fast uppercut caught the brave under his chin and snapped back his head, causing him to drop to the ground like a heavy sack of spuds where he lay unconscious.

Hearing hoof beats behind him, Ethan turned to face two more Sioux warriors racing up to him carrying lances which they flung at him when they came within range. Still shaken from his battle with the knife-wielding brave, Jackson was slow in dodging the spears and one of them opened up a gash on his right side which began to bleed profusely.

Dropping to the ground, Ethan rolled to the left, dodging the ponies' hooves as the Indians tried to ride their horses over him. The two warriors were confident, for they were mounted and had an unarmed wounded white man outnumbered two to one. That was a big mistake, for Jackson was a root-hog-or-die kind of a fighter.

Picking up the unconscious brave's knife, Ethan threw it at the nearest red man's chest, where it stuck and unseated the hapless rider from his horse. But it was the second rider whose luck really left him, for Jackson had spotted his lost Colt lying on the ground not more than ten feet away. Diving for the weapon, he rolled and came up firing the revolver, rendering another pony riderless.

After securely tying the unconscious brave to a tree, Ethan replaced the spent shells in his Colt. Knowing that the white-man smell would spook the Indian ponies, he didn't bother trying to catch them; instead he set out on foot for Fort Laramie.

Walking mostly at night and taking the time to cover his tracks, it was a full six days before Jackson arrived—footsore and weary—at Fort Laramie.

Standing near the graveyard located on the hill outside the fort, Jackson noticed that Johnson's wagons had finally arrived. He figured that Collins had moved out about two days before and, as soon as he outfitted himself with some gear and a new horse, he'd be joining him.

As he started down the hill he figured on saying howdy to Johnson and heading on out for Oregon. Noticing a newly dug grave and being curious by nature, he stopped to read the epitaph carved on the wooden headstone. It read: *Tom Johnson, 1826–1876. Kilt by injuns.*

Chapter Four
Joining Up

The death of Tom Johnson had been a shock, and when Jackson saw that Collins hadn't left the fort—he was downright perplexed.

Jake Collins was talking to a group of people from Johnson's train when he spotted Ethan walking into the fort. Jim Cooper, who had also spotted the former sheriff, said, "All right Collins, there's Jackson, ask him."

A crowd started to follow Collins as he walked toward Jackson, but he stopped them by holding up his hand and saying, "Just hold on there folks. If'n you all will remember, you kicked that man off your train and I don't figure he's forgot that. It's best if I talk to him in private. So why don't all of you sort of make yourselves scarce for awhile." Then, looking at Jim Cooper, he said, " 'Specially you, Cooper!"

Taking Collins's advice, the crowd dispersed, with most of them returning to their own wagons.

Walking up to Jackson, Jake stuck out his hand and asked, "You and your horse have a fallin' out, or you just fall off?"

Shaking Collins's hand, Ethan said, "Me and the Sioux had us a little disagreement up in the Big Horns and my horse didn't hang around to see how things turned out."

"Sound judgement on his part," observed Collins. And then, in hushed tones, Jake said, "Your horse showed up here several days ago. Don't worry, everything was still on him—including the gold. I hid it in the wagon." Being a prospector himself, and knowing it was considered bad manners to ask another man about his business, Jake couldn't keep from asking the next question. "Was it a big strike?"

"Real big," answered Ethan. "But until just now I figured the only things I got out of the mountains with was my handgun and hide."

"Real big, huh?" asked Jake.

"Big enough to share with some friends who've got enough nerve to follow me the next time I head back there. That includes you if you're interested."

Smiling, Jake said, "Sonny, the day I ain't interested in gold is the day they'll be a throwin' dirt over me."

"Well, things are a bit too hot in the mountains right now to do any prospecting, but as soon as things quiet down some and we get established in Oregon we can head back here with some good men and clean out this place I found. For right now, though, we need to get to Oregon— speaking of which, why are you still here and not on the trail?"

"The army won't let us leave the fort. It seems like that idjit Custer got himself massacred on the Little Big Horn and now the army's afraid to let us civilians out of their sight. Seems they're afraid we might get massacred ourselves."

"We can't stay here," Jackson said. "If we don't leave pretty soon the snow will have the mountain passes blocked and we'll be stuck here using up our supplies. By the time the snows start to melt in the spring all our stores will be drained to the point where we won't have enough supplies left to get established in Oregon, not to mention the fact that people can't travel without supplies."

"Well, you know how the military is," Jake said. "They ain't known for their long-range thinking—or thinking at all as far as that goes."

Shaking his head, Jackson glanced toward Johnson's wagon train and asked, "How is it that Tom Johnson ended up getting killed?"

"Some of his dang fool greenhorns got him killed," answered Jake.

"How'd it happen?"

"You remember that idjit, Jim Cooper?"

"Yeah."

"Well, him and two other fools figured they'd take to huntin' Injuns for sport. Seems they figure the red man to be nothin' more than some sort of a wild animal and as such it's all right to hunt 'em. So they got themselves up a little huntin' party and started takin' potshots at some Sioux a headin' up north. Of course, the Sioux didn't take too kindly to all that and attacked the wagon train to get even—Johnson got killed in the attack and a few of the settlers got banged up a mite in the fracas, but not one of the men who started all the trouble got so much as a scratch. How you figure that?"

"Sounds about right," Jackson said. "Who were the other two fools?"

"Lonnie Leary and a man named Aaron Stark."

"I noticed Cooper talking to you when I walked in— what kind of a burr he got under his saddle?"

Clearing his throat, Jake said, "I reckon that's one of the peculiar things about life that makes it so downright interesting at times. It seems that with Tom gone the greenhorns need a new guide and wagon boss and they want me for the job."

"What'd you tell them?"

"Told 'em I already had a job workin' for you, but then they come back at me and offered to let you join back up with 'em if'n you'd agree to let me act as guide for everybody."

"Mighty generous of them," commented Ethan, sarcastically.

"I told 'em I'd make the offer," said Collins. "What do you want me to tell 'em?"

Thinking for a bit, Ethan said, "Tell them I'll let them know tonight."

Ethan was tired and footsore from his long walk; all he wanted just then was to take a bath, have a good meal, and sleep for the rest of the day. He'd make his decision after he rested and ate.

It was almost dark before Jackson awakened. Putting on his boots, he set off for the commandant's office.

The man in charge of the post was a major named Clayton Frederick—a career officer of little ability and even less imagination. His bible was the army manual and his favorite phrase was "Orders are orders."

Jackson was finding it almost impossible to get through to the thick-headed major. He'd laid out the situation for the officer in detail—emphasizing all the important points—but all Frederick would do was quote regulations and show Jackson a copy of his orders which stated he was to detain anyone traveling on the Oregon Trail. And that was exactly what the major planned on doing until further orders were issued.

Tired of trying to use logic, Ethan tried appealing to Frederick's sense of self-preservation when he pointed out to him that there were people on the wagon trains who were desperate enough to defy his authority and push ahead. What would his soldiers do then—shoot the settlers? That wouldn't go over too well back in Washington. And what would happen to the major's authority at the post if he allowed his orders to be disobeyed? It seemed like a no-win kind of situation to Ethan.

Finally understanding Ethan's logic, the major agreed to let anyone who wanted to leave the protection of the fort do so. As a matter of fact, he was relieved to be rid of the civilians—they were extremely undisciplined and had no respect for orders whatsoever.

Leaving the major's office, Ethan headed for the wagons where all the people had gathered in anticipation of what he was going to say concerning the possibility of the separate groups coming together to form one wagon train.

A middle-aged man of medium height left the group to greet Jackson. "Hello Mr. Jackson, my name's Emitt Lawson, and I've been chosen to speak for our group. Would you care to discuss the situation?"

The man was straightforward and looked Jackson in the eye—Ethan liked that about him. So he decided to be straightforward with the man. "No need for a representative and no need for any discussions. I'm well aware of how things stand—probably better aware than any of the people in your group. I'll just speak my peace and let you folks decide what you want to do."

"All right," said Lawson.

Climbing to the seat of a nearby wagon, Ethan cleared his throat and launched into his speech. "It's my understanding that you folks from Johnson's wagon train have invited me to rejoin you on the trip to Oregon. I am well aware that the invitation was only extended so you could secure the services of Jake Collins as guide and wagon boss."

There was a murmuring among the people but no one offered to dispute what had been said.

"I'm not going to bother trying to explain the actions that caused you people to oust me from your group—you haven't been in the country long enough to understand how things work out here. So I'm just going to tell you how things stand—it'll save a lot of time and trouble."

Taking a breath, Ethan continued, "To begin with, I have no intention of joining your group."

That statement got everybody's attention and caused an immediate uproar and protest.

When the noise abated, Jackson continued, "On the other hand, I will allow you to follow along behind my group—for the simple reason that we will be providing each other with protection. As to how the trains will be run, our group is run by a committee made up of myself, John Baldwin, and Caleb Kenton—you folks can run yours to suit yourselves. But neither group can tell the other what to do—and anyone is free to leave any time he pleases."

Pausing to let what he'd said sink in, Ethan waited a couple of minutes before he continued. "We'll be leaving in the morning at first light. My wagon will be in the lead—follow or stay behind."

There was quite a lively debate for a few minutes until a vote was held among what was now Lawson's people during which it was decided that the terms Jackson had laid down were acceptable.

Lawson walked over to Ethan and extended his hand. "Agreed," he said.

After Jackson and Lawson had shaken hands, Collins moved up beside Ethan and quietly asked, "Think this little get-together will work out?"

Checking to see that he wasn't heard, Ethan answered, "No chance of it working. I only let them join up with us because there are some good people among them and with a little luck, I'm sort of hoping that they might have a better chance with us there to help them—and twenty-one wagons does make a harder target."

"It makes a richer prize too," observed Collins.

Chapter Five
Leantown

The trail leading to Oregon was proving to be longer and harder to travel than Ethan had at first thought. Four weeks on the road had been cursed by numerous breakdowns, bad weather, Indian attacks, and night raids by marauding animals filling their bellies on settler's livestock.

Right then, due to an Indian attack that had forced them to remain at Fort Laramie for two weeks, they were three weeks behind schedule, with a good chance that snow had already blocked off the mountain passes. And even if that weren't the case, there was always the possibility of getting caught in a storm while trying to go through the pass and ending up trapped in the mountains.

And while nature and hostiles were doing a good job of hampering their progress, Lonnie Leary and his poor excuse for a wagon would have had to have been given first prize if awards were being handed out for slowing them down. For it was a rare day that one of the wagons in Lawson's group wasn't being cannibalized to patch up the "Leary coach" so it could keep on rolling.

So while they'd only been on the road for four weeks,

everybody was relieved when they saw the buildings of a settlement appear in the sheltered valley below them. The sign outside of town announced that they were now entering *Leantown: population 43*. Ethan noted that when the wagon train rolled into the settlement, its population would more than double.

As he neared the buildings, Ethan began to understand how Leantown had got its name. There were only ten buildings scattered about forming the community. Most of the structures were just ramshackle affairs showing little pride in ownership. Only one building on the trail spoke of any traffic; at least there were two horses tied to the hitching rail outside of it. Jackson figured that it was probably what passed for the town saloon and drove his wagon toward the building. When he stopped by the hitching post there was a welcoming committee waiting for him which consisted of two old men and a flop-eared dog.

"Howdy," said the youngest of the two, whose age Ethan guessed to be hovering close to sixty.

"Howdy," replied Jackson. "I reckon things don't get really lively around here 'till Saturday night."

The older gent spoke. "Son, if you ever wake up and find that things have gotten lively—you can be sure of one thing—you ain't in this town."

Both old men laughed and Ethan chuckled at the joke.

Everybody would have liked to go inside the building, but the makeshift saloon could only accommodate ten people at one time, so only the leaders of the wagon trains and the towns leading citizens met inside. And it was there that Ethan's worst fear was realized—word had reached town that the mountain passes had been blocked by an early snow.

So there it was—it was too late to cross the mountains, and, as usual, no one could agree on what to do next. Not that they had that many choices—turn back or stay put were their only options. Of course there were a few who refused to believe that the passes were blocked. After all, it was still August and the sun was shining—how could anything be snowed in? Of course, there were plenty of people around who tried to explain to them that the weather in the mountains was different from what they were used to in the East. But the people who were arguing to go on were the type of folks who had to be shown they were wrong if they disagreed with what they were told—nothing would do but for them to see for themselves if the pass was blocked.

Collins made the observation that not only had the train started out from Missouri but apparently many of the people traveling on it hailed from the "show-me-state."

Of course nobody chose to turn back. After all, if they'd had anything worthwhile back where they'd started from, they wouldn't have left in the first place.

So, in the end, five wagons kept on heading west despite the advice and dire warnings given to them about what lay ahead of them and that they very well might not make it out alive if they went too high into the mountains. But they were proud and arrogant people who were certain they knew more about the weather in the mountains than people who had lived in the country all of their lives. They were so sure of themselves that they were not only willing to bet their own lives but risk the lives of their families just to prove that they were superior to a bunch of cowardly ignorant westerners.

Unfortunate, at least in Jackson's opinion, was the fact that they had refused to include Leary and Jim Cooper in their group when they were putting together their wagon train.

As for himself, Ethan planned on wintering where he

was. With that goal in mind, he set to building a cabin for himself and Collins so they could wait out the winter in relative comfort.

The others, including those in what remained of Lawson's group, followed his example and set to work building their own cabins. Within a month, what was once a languishing community of forty-three souls was now a growing community of almost twice that size.

The original settlers had also been on their way to Oregon when a lack of supplies and bad weather forced them to stop and establish what they now called Leantown. And while they had intended to move on in the spring, they had become trapped: lacking the supplies to move on or go back, they remained in the valley where they traded with the Indians and travelers passing through. After five years, all of the supplies were gone and fewer and fewer wagon trains were coming through with which they could trade. Soon the town would be nothing but a memory. With the hunters having to go farther each year to find game with which to sustain them through the harsh winters, that time was not far away.

While the town had been finding it hard to survive, with the arrival of Jackson and the others, it was once again beginning to show signs of life. All things considered, Leantown was a nice place to settle down and raise children. But the community lacked something vital for any town—it desperately needed some sort of industry to keep it going. Mining, farming, logging were all prospects, but Leantown had none of those activities.

The growing season at that altitude was much too short to allow farming. There had been no gold or silver found in large enough amounts for commercial mining, and while there were trees, there was no easy way of getting them to market. Looking at the situation with a hard eye, Jackson couldn't see any way the town could survive; he considered it a shame, for it was just the type of town he was looking to settle down in.

There were only two places in town that showed any signs of life at all—the saloon and what passed for the general store. The store was run by a comely young widow by the name of Sharon O'Brien and her ten-year-old son, Corey. The store, unlike most such places found in less isolated parts of the territory, carried a large supply of furs and homemade goods instead of the usual flour, nails, and leather goods common to such establishments.

It hadn't always been that way, for when the store first went into business five years before it was well stocked. But as time went by the original supply of goods customarily found in such places such as flour, beans, nails, and horseshoes began to dwindle away and were replaced with the furs and goods with which the shelves were now stacked.

There was also a shortage of hard cash in town, and with there being no nearby authority to print up script the people could exchange with each other, the only currency that existed was a pinch of gold dust, or what most people had been using since the beginning of time—bartering.

To the residents of Leantown, the folks on the wagon train looked downright well-to-do, with their store-bought clothes and canned goods, not to mention the fact that the travelers carried something as scarce as hen's teeth in those parts—cash money. While Ethan had goods with which to barter and cash, he planned on holding on to both. Especially since he was carrying three sacks of gold in his wagon. He planned to use that when purchasing goods in town.

But how to go about using the ore to bargain with? Everybody he'd been traveling with from Fort Laramie knew he'd been prospecting in the Big Horn Mountains, and while he planned to return to the mountains with an expedition in the spring, he didn't want to lead a parade of people to his "glory hole."

Ethan brought up the subject with Jake, the only other person who knew about his find and, as usual—when it came to matters requiring a certain amount of secrecy— Collins had an answer for the problem vexing his employer.

"Ain't nothin' a keepin' you from prospectin' around here, is there?" he asked.

"No," replied Jackson. "But that don't mean I'll be able to find any gold around Leantown; how's that gonna help me?"

"Son, until gold is melted into bars and stamped there ain't no kind of identifyin' marks on it. So who's to say that gold you got squirreled away in the wagon didn't come from some creek around here?"

Understanding what the wily old mountain man was getting at, Ethan grinned and said, "I'm beginning to understand how you managed to stay alive all those years you were living in the mountains. I guess you could figure your way out of pretty much any kind of a difficulty."

"Just about," agreed Jake.

So it was decided that Ethan was to go exploring the next day: do some hunting and fishing, and sometime during the foray he would discover there was gold in the area.

With winter just around the corner, most folks thought it was foolish for Ethan to go traipsing off when Collins would be needing help with the cabin and cutting firewood in preparation for what could be one of the brutal winters Wyoming was famous for.

But Ethan wasn't concerned about what people thought of his habits or judgement; he only cared about whether or not they believed he'd found gold on his trip. With that in

mind, he noted the location of creeks and other likely looking places about which he could drop hints to the folks
when they asked him about the location of his claim—and
while most people were too polite to ask questions about
such matters, there were plenty of folks from Lawson's
train who didn't share that virtue.

Having found a creek by late afternoon that looked like
it might contain gold, Ethan dismounted and went through
the motions of panning out some ore. He was careful to
leave plenty of evidence of his work for those who were
certain to try and figure out where he'd been mining when
word got out about his strike.

Figuring he'd done enough of the fake work to fool those
who would follow his path, Ethan spent the rest of the day
hunting and within an hour he was riding with a buck mule
deer draped across his saddle. Riding along, Jackson was
relaxed but alert—alert enough to spot the Indian watching
him from a distant ridge. Digging into his saddlebag, Ethan
brought out a pair of field glasses and used them to get a
better look at who was observing him.

Immediately he recognized the watcher to be a member
of the Sioux tribe; he also recognized him to be the warrior
he'd left tied to a tree in the Big Horns.

That night Ethan mulled things over in his mind but
could think of no logical reason that would explain why
that Sioux warrior was hanging around outside of Leantown. And while it worried him a mite, he hadn't men-
tioned it to anybody when he brought in the deer and
handed it over to Collins who set to cutting it up and dis-
tributing it among Kenton and Baldwin.

Pushing his concern about the Indian from his mind,
Ethan began to think about how he should go about getting
word out concerning his "discovery." He finally came to

the conclusion that the best way was to spend some of the gold in the general store.

Sharon O'Brien was a pleasant woman of about twenty-five years of age. It was a disposition that the people who knew her story found hard to understand. After all, she'd lost her husband to a fever not long after they'd begun their westward trek and had been forced to open the store her husband had hoped to start and run it by herself.

Contracting others to put up the building, she'd been running the enterprise ever since they had first arrived at what they ended up calling Leantown.

Ethan admired the young woman's nerve; he also admired her looks. At five-ten and with long black hair, she was a strikingly beautiful woman. And Jackson had no doubt that she wouldn't have been lacking for suitors in whatever part of the territory she chose to settle in.

Forcing his attention back to the matter at hand, Ethan began to pick up a few items. He regretted having to mislead the beautiful Mrs. O'Brien, but it couldn't be helped. Placing the items he'd chosen on the counter, he reached into the leather sack at his side and took out a pinch of gold dust to pay for them.

Sharon O'Brien openly gasped when she saw the yellow metal—but then she recovered enough to bring out the scales she kept under the counter. "Haven't had to use these around here for quite a while," she said as she manipulated the weights and began handing back small increments of the dust until the scales balanced perfectly.

Seeing the care the young woman used to make sure she gave him a fair measure made Jackson cringe when he thought about the lie he was going to tell her when she asked about where the gold came from. But Sharon had lived long enough in the west to know that you didn't ask a prospector about the location of his claim. She was curious but she held her tongue.

Ethan was both relieved and disappointed in not being asked about his supposed strike; relieved in that he wouldn't have to lie to Sharon O'Brien, and disappointed in the fact that he was sure that Mrs. O'Brien would remain tight-lipped about his gold.

Knowing he would have to find another means of getting word out about his strike, he said good-bye to Sharon and left for his wagon. After careful consideration, Jackson decided to use Collins as his means of announcing his find, and when he approached Jake with his plan, he found a willing participant in his scheme.

During the journey from Missouri the people in Johnson's wagon train had gotten into the habit of having social get-togethers on occasion, and some of the men always ended the festivities with a poker game. At least that was the way things had started out; now there was a whole lot less socializing and much more card playing—and the frequency of the games had increased to the point where there appeared one was occurring almost every night. That is, unless the wives could harangue their husbands into staying at home—which had been known to happen on occasion.

Jackson had never participated in the games himself, but his group was well represented by Jake Collins, who it seems was not only bitten by the gold bug but the gambling bug as well. And it was through that addiction that Ethan planned to let the news of his strike slip out.

At a rough-hewn table inside the saloon, ten men were gathered: four card players and six observers. The players were Collins, Jim Cooper, Aaron Stark, and a young man in his early twenties named Phillip Jenkins.

Jenkins, who had been recently married, had had his first marital spat with his wife and had ended it by stomping off in anger when she, after having exhausted all other forms of persuasion, had finally forbidden him to go to the game. Of course when she did that it was like waving a red flag in front of a bull; Jenkins had to go to the game then to prove he still wore the pants in the family if nothing else.

They had all been playing cards for about an hour; during that hour Collins's poke had been getting lighter while his skill as a poker player decreased with every drink of whiskey he was throwing down his throat.

In truth Jake was a pretty fair hand when it came to handling cards—drunk or sober—and was actually having a hard time losing to the incompetent Cooper and Stark. Jake couldn't say as to whether Jenkins was any good at poker or not—he was obviously preoccupied with something and as a result of that he was playing a pretty lousy hand.

It took another hour of hard work losing to the incompetent players until Collins felt justified in digging out the quarter-ounce nugget and laying it on the table.

"That ought to cover the bet, boys," he said, slurring his words.

It was everything Collins could do to keep from laughing out loud when he saw how their jaws dropped when their eyes fell on that glittering nugget.

Cooper was the first to recover enough to ask the question.

"Where'd you get that?"

Pretending to be drunk, Jake answered, "Part of my wages. Ethan found it in one of the creeks around here."

Motioning for everyone to move in closer, Jake belched and said in hushed tones, "Told me not to tell nobody 'bout where he found it. But you old boys ain't gonna be a tellin' nobody are ya?" Jake had pretended to whisper but everybody in the room had heard him and all of them were shaking their heads in agreement that they wouldn't be telling a soul about Ethan's find. As soon as the final hand was played, with Cooper winning the nugget, the room cleared, every man making a beeline for his home.

By the afternoon of the next day there wasn't a man, woman, or child who hadn't heard about the bonanza that had been struck in their backyard.

A month later the wagons started to arrive. They came loaded with lumber to build sluice boxes to wash out the gold; they came loaded with shovels, picks, and gold pans. One wagon came loaded with nothing but flour. Another brought chickens. Stories had been floating around about how a man could get rich digging in the dirt for gold or he could dig in the miners' pockets for gold by providing him with something he needed after a hard day prospecting.

Along with the speculators and merchants came the thieves, gamblers, and dance hall girls eager and primed to separate the miner from his gold with the turn of a card or a pretty smile.

The temperature had turned cold, but property in and around Leantown was selling for prices that were really warming things up, and all of the original settlers, including the Lawson and Collins's wagon train members who had bought land when it was cheap, were basking in their new-found prosperity. Of course, that didn't include Jake and Ethan, who were making themselves scarce around town and couldn't leave the city limits without being followed by eager prospectors hoping they would lead them to where Jackson had made his strike.

They were both more than a little nervous and feeling a bit guilty, since they were responsible for a hoax that had caused folks to pull up stakes and leave their homes and businesses to head off on some "wild goose chase," hunting for gold where none had been found. Both Jake and Ethan felt that they could easily end up dancing on the ends of some ropes if people ever found out what had really happened.

Ethan couldn't believe that one lie could produce so much activity. And instead of being reviled by the local people—he was looked upon as something of a savior. After all, they did own most of the land in the area and were getting rich by selling small parcels to the newcomers.

And Sharon O'Brien was very happy about how things were turning out. She had made deals with most of the new merchants arriving in town to handle their goods or had rented them out lots on which they could set up their own establishments. It seemed that it didn't matter what she tried she couldn't help but make money.

Sharon had bought the chickens and the wagon filled with flour outright with some of the money she'd been paid by the merchants and had opened up a restaurant that was doing a land office business—it was doing so well that Jake had decided to go into business with her in the enterprise and not only became a full partner in the eatery but the head cook as well.

Even though Collins was enjoying the new business, he agreed with Jackson that once spring arrived and the people started prospecting in earnest, it was best that they be nowhere near Leantown when the folks finally figured out that there was no gold around the settlement.

Jackson hadn't gone prospecting since that first time, and while he worried that that might make people suspicious, most of them figured he was afraid someone might follow him and discover where he'd made his strike—and since he couldn't get all of the gold out quickly that must mean that there was a lot of it to dig out. Ethan thought it was funny how once some folks got an idea they wanted to believe inside their heads, it didn't matter what happened to disprove that notion, folks went right on believing what they wanted to.

There was no doubt that Ethan had gotten himself into a real mess and he didn't have any idea about how to get out of it. He could tell folks about the gold he'd found in the Big Horn Mountains—but would they believe him about that? Would they want to follow him into an area infested with the warlike Sioux, or would they be just as happy to string him up in Leantown and be done with it? Given his reputation, Ethan figured the hangman's noose would get the nod if it came to that.

Such were his thoughts while he stood in Sharon O'Brien's store that day and an out-of-breath newcomer ran through the door. Taking a few seconds to catch his breath, the man announced, "Gold! They've found gold on Hard Luck Creek not more than two miles from town!"

Chapter Six
Prosperity

The activity in and around Leantown had been steadily increasing with each passing day, but after the discovery of gold at Hard Luck Creek, things around the settlement really got hectic. Prospectors and other types of "gold diggers" were putting up tents wherever they could find a space not already occupied—some didn't even observe that convention of civilized behavior, and a man who left his camp unattended for the briefest period might return to find his tent collapsed and pushed aside and a larger party of men occupying his former space. Where once cash had been a scarce commodity in Leantown, money now flowed like water during a spring flood.

Every day that the weather would permit it miners were panning out shovels full of dirt retrieved from the icy water, and those who hadn't yet found "color" were running to and fro dipping their pans into any place they could find where the water hadn't turned to ice; even in spots where the streams had frozen over men were breaking through the ice with axes and sledgehammers and building fires on the banks to warm their hands when they became too stiff to use a shovel or a gold pan.

Some of the men would work in the icy water until their hands turned blue and then rush to the fire to warm them until they turned a more natural shade of pink or red and then rush right back to the stream to continue their work.

Word continued to spread about the strike, and when the snow got too deep for wagons and all but the largest and strongest of horses to muscle their way through the snow to the settlement, people started to arrive on skis and snow-shoes wearing packs on their backs.

Jake was happy to hear that someone other than Ethan had found gold in the area, but being suspicious by nature, the mountain man had asked his employer if he had "salted" the creek with his own gold to take the heat off himself when more ore wasn't found. Jackson admitted that if he had thought of salting the creek he probably would have, but as far as he knew, the strike had been legitimate and Leantown had been growing by leaps and bounds of its own volition.

While the population of the community was increasing, the new residents weren't exactly those who one would choose to make up a community of law-abiding citizens. Most of the new arrivals were miners and folks who thought that the only thing they had to do to get rich was walk around and pick up fist-size nuggets lying on the ground—they were sheep waiting to be sheared. And along with the sheep came the wolves eager to prey on them.

But, as with all civilized folk, it wasn't long before they began to get organized and started making plans to bring law and order to their growing town.

The predators, who had staked out Leantown as their own, weren't about to let a group of people made up mostly of tenderfeet from back East run them off their hunting grounds, however. As quickly as the good citizens could get together to decide on a course of action designed to clean up the town, they were harassed, beaten, and run off before the meeting could even be called to order.

The only people who hadn't been harassed were those in Collins's group, the reason being that they were the type of citizens who tended to get downright "salty" when dealing with the criminal element in the community, and were getting to be known as the kind of folks who it was best to leave alone. Even John Baldwin, after spending time under Jackson's tutelage, was becoming known as something of a gun hand. The former school teacher had already shot two renegades who had made the mistake of thinking that the mild-mannered scholar was just another easy victim for them to prey upon. And while his skill with a Colt increased with each lesson he took from Jackson, he also showed good judgement when it came to dealing with people. Ethan commented that if he'd been planning to wear a badge again he would have picked Baldwin for a deputy without hesitation—not that he figured he'd ever be working as a lawman again or that John would ever be foolish enough to pin on a badge.

Caleb Kenton was another man in the group who had bark on him, but instead of getting involved in disputes, he preferred to work and supervise his two eldest sons in the construction of homes and shelters for the new arrivals so they would have a roof over their heads when the weather turned mean.

Caleb and his sons had started quite a construction business among themselves and had even begun hiring other people to work for them. Kenton remarked that he had gone to bed one night a Kentucky hillbilly and woke up the next morning a Wyoming businessman. The rest of the Kenton children, along with the two Baldwin offspring, were finding employment doing odd jobs around town, for the settlement was booming and growing at a rate the original settlers wouldn't have dreamed possible a month earlier.

On that Wednesday night at Ethan Jackson's cabin there were no smiling faces, nor any jovial men slapping each other on the back congratulating each other on their good fortune. But there were plenty of worried looks on the faces of the town's leading citizens. News of the meeting and its location had been kept secret for fear of it being broken up by some of the toughs who it appeared were now running the town—not even Jackson had known that he was going to be visited. If he had known about what those assembled were about to suggest, he would have been even more surprised.

Emitt Lawson, as usual, was the first to speak. "Ethan, the citizens of this community—at least the honest ones—have been meeting trying to figure out how to get back control of our town from the lowlifes who have taken over. The majority of us think we need a sheriff. Somebody who has worked as a town tamer—somebody like you. We want you to be the sheriff of Leantown."

Jackson was completely taken aback by the offer and could only stand there, speechless. Not so long ago he had been told by most of these same men that he was too violent to travel with them to Oregon; now they wanted him to wear a badge and put his life on the line to protect them and their property. It never failed to amaze Ethan how fast people could change their minds about something when it was to their benefit to do so.

But while Jackson was silently contemplating what had been said and was refraining from chastising his traveling companions for their hypocritical attitudes, Jake Collins had no problem speaking up and letting those assembled know what he thought of them. "If'n that don't go and beat all I've ever seen in my life," he said, taking off his hat and slapping it against his leg. "Back in Missouri most of you folks couldn't wait to get rid of this man and now here you go a wantin' him to put his life on the line to protect your property and your sorry hides!"

Nobody disputed what Collins had said, although some would have liked to for many of them were the type who considered themselves to always be right.

"Everybody has agreed to contribute to a fund that your salary will be paid from," said Lawson. "It comes to a tidy sum that will probably match or beat what you were paid in some of the cow towns you've worked in," he added.

When Ethan didn't answer immediately, Jim Cooper became impatient and said, "We're offering you a hundred dollars a month—you can't turn that down." Cooper thrust out his chin to make his point, a gesture that sorely tempted Kenton to once again take a swing at him.

Jackson only smiled and said, "Money don't have anything to do with the reason I became a lawman, and it has nothing to do with the reason I'm turning down your offer now. You see, the reason I was headed for Oregon in the first place was to find somewhere I could get away from my reputation as a 'town tamer.' If I took the job you want me to take I'd not only be dragging along my unwanted reputation but adding to it every time I was forced to face somebody in the street. So my pulling up stakes and traveling all this way would be for nothing—would you be willing to do that?"

There was a general din among the men as they jostled among themselves for position in the tightly packed cabin until Lawson quieted the room enough so he could ask Ethan another question. "What about all the thievin' and killin' that's been going on? What are we supposed to do— wait for some of those thieves to break down our doors and rob us at their leisure?"

"Nope," answered Ethan. "There's no question that what's been going on has got to stop. All I'm saying is that I don't intend to take the lead in doing what has to be done since that would only bring unwanted attention on me and the town as well. I'm not saying I won't lend a hand when it comes to cleaning up Leantown—I will. But only as an advisor. Pick somebody else for sheriff, make sure you hire enough deputies to help him get the job done, and make sure that all of you stand with the man you pick for the job. Do that and your problems with the rowdier element in town will soon disappear."

"But who do we pick for a sheriff? Nobody among us is a gunfighter . . . except for you," said Lawson.

"That's true," agreed Jackson. "But being good with a gun isn't the most important thing you look for in a good lawman. Good judgement is more important than a fast gun any day of the week."

There were a couple of minutes of muted conversation as the people inside the cabin debated the situation among themselves. During a lull in the debate Jim Cooper called for everyone's attention and said, "I nominate Lonnie Leary for sheriff of Leantown."

Several people in the room gasped at the suggestion and a couple of them laughed out loud at what Cooper had said. But Jackson was tempted to remain silent and let the big man try wearing a badge for a while—if the citizens of Leantown were so foolish as to appoint him to that office. Ethan figured that within a week Sheriff Leary would either be shot or run out of town on a rail. But eventually his sense of duty forced him to speak out concerning the situation. "There's only one man in this town who has the skills and judgement to be sheriff of Leantown, if he's foolish enough to take the job, that is."

"Who would that be?" asked Lawson.

"John Baldwin," answered Jackson.

A stunned silence fell over the room, at least for a few seconds, until Emitt Lawson spoke up. "But Baldwin's a schoolteacher, not a gunman," he protested. "And as far as I know he's never been a lawman of any kind before."

"True," agreed Jackson. "But with everybody here backing him up he's plenty good enough with a gun to get the job done."

"But he don't have any kind of a reputation at all," said Cooper. "People will be showing up from all over the territory just to take a shot at our 'kid sheriff.' "

"Nope. Just the opposite as a matter of fact—a strong law-and-order town that relies on a lot of peace officers to keep control of the lawless will be avoided and shunned by gunfighters. If only one man ran this town and relied on his reputation to keep order, well the type of man who wants a reputation as a gunman would break his neck trying to get here. Take my advice and hire plenty of men to enforce the law—it'll be a lot cheaper in the long run. Besides, think about how tame this town will sound after word gets around that a schoolteacher can keep order in it."

The meeting continued for awhile with Baldwin standing around in something of a daze. He hadn't even given any thought to becoming a lawman—he was a schoolteacher and a farmer; he wasn't the type of man who went around bashing drunks on the head and throwing them in jail cells. He couldn't imagine whatever had possessed Ethan to recommend him for the job.

It took awhile, but things finally quieted down enough so Lawson could ask the reluctant schoolteacher if he would take the job as town sheriff. Despite serious misgivings about his qualifications to hold such a post, John was a public-minded citizen who felt compelled to do his duty when called upon by his fellow citizens, so he reluctantly accepted the appointment.

Cheers erupted, and after Baldwin shook the hand of every man in the room who was eager to congratulate him, Lawson called the meeting to order once again. They then set about electing a town council and a mayor to govern the settlement.

While there was a natural inclination to hold an open election and allow everyone in town to vote, those assembled took note of the fact that they were meeting in secret as it was so that they could make choices of how to run the town without being harassed by the lawless element that was now running things. If they put the matter to a public vote the criminals in town would threaten and intimidate the honest citizens of Leantown and bribe the rest until they ended up stealing the election and putting their people in office. The result being that they would end up governed by a duly elected body of thieves and cutthroats determined to pick the honest citizens' pockets.

With that in mind, the people in attendance in the cabin decided to pick a mayor and town council from those who were there assembled. Those chosen were Emitt Lawson, mayor; Phillip Jenkins, original founding member of Leantown and now a council member; and Jake Collins, council member.

The mayor and council members all agreed to serve without pay, but the sheriff and his three regular deputies were to be paid a salary. The sheriff was to be paid $100 a month and each of his deputies would be paid $50 a month for risking their lives. A special tax, if necessary, was to be levied to pay their salaries.

Jackson assured them that the fines levied against folks running afoul of the law—at least during the first few months—would be more than enough to cover the lawmen's salaries for quite some time. The tax, then, would probably not have to be instituted, and if it were, the rate would be very low—a financial arrangement highly favored by the tax-paying, law-abiding citizens.

The next morning Jackson met with Baldwin and his deputies, all of whom were sporting brand-new badges on their chests, courtesy of the local blacksmith. And even though Ethan wasn't being paid to teach the new lawmen his profession, he was being very thorough in his instruction and would end up teaching them many of the tricks he'd learned—most of them the hard way—that had helped him to stay alive during his many years of working some of the roughest towns on the frontier.

Remembering that he had once seen Baldwin use a staff while walking over rough ground, and how deftly he had once used it to dispatch a rattlesnake that had crossed his path, Ethan made a gift of a cane he had taken to carrying since some miscreant, unhappy at being arrested, had shot him in the leg, forcing him to use the stick to help him walk his rounds for a couple of months. During that time, Ethan had found the varnished hickory walking stick with its heavy ornate silver handle and blunt brass tip to be not only useful in helping support his wounded leg, but to be much more effective than a fist when applied to the skull of someone who wasn't all that deserving of being shot but was too stubborn or stupid to be reasoned with.

The cane had not only proven itself to be an effective form of persuasion. Jackson had also found that it could be used as a distraction when he'd been forced to face someone determined to engage him in a gunfight to prove how brave he was—most of the time, some kid ended up proving how hard it was to control one's bodily functions while staring down the barrel of a cocked .45.

On several occasions Ethan had found that either by gesturing or spinning the walking stick his opponent's attention was irresistibly drawn to the cane, giving Ethan enough time to draw and fire with such accuracy that the gunslinger ended up being wounded instead of having to be buried on some "boot hill."

On one occasion Jackson had purposely let the cane fall to the ground, with his opponent becoming so fascinated by the falling stick that he followed its path all the way to the dusty street, giving Ethan enough time to draw and level his revolver at the stunned gunman's chest before he could even start to draw his sidearm.

After telling his students that tale, Jackson regaled them with a couple more stories designed to teach them how to handle sticky situations that had a tendency to crop up in the law enforcement business. He then led them out of town on horseback, where he set to teaching them some gun handling techniques that many would-be gunslingers would have given their non-gun-handling arms to learn—especially since the tricks were being taught by someone as famous as Ethan Jackson.

Finally, Ethan dismissed his class early that evening with the admonition to try and get some rest, for he knew they would be undergoing their baptism of fire that night when they set out to enforce the law. And all of them knew that things were apt to turn lively when the rowdier element was introduced to the fact that the law had come to Leantown.

A new and much more spacious saloon had just opened up in the settlement, and with its greater supply of whiskey it also boasted a rough and lawless clientele who were prone to be found wherever trouble started. It was in that establishment John planned to introduce himself and his deputies.

At ten that night Baldwin strolled into the Gold Star

Saloon. He was nattily dressed in a broadcloth suit and a flat-crowned hat—clothes he generally wore while teaching school back in Ohio. He wore a coat buttoned at the front which hid the badge pinned to his shirt and the Colt stuck in his waistband. His deputies followed behind him wearing longer coats that hid the Greener shotguns they had tucked under their arms.

Being a mild-mannered man and so neatly dressed among men who were so roughly dressed was just asking for trouble, but it was still early by saloon standards and the patrons of the Gold Star had yet to imbibe enough rot-gut to get them started expressing their annoyance with something by taking shots at it.

Baldwin and his deputies had all taken up strategic locations in the saloon and were waiting for the first fight to break out. There were also several unpaid official deputies scattered about who were ready to expose their badges and help out if Baldwin were to need them. The only prominent citizen who wasn't to be seen at the time was Ethan Jackson. He'd declined to put on a badge and join them, saying that Baldwin had to take the lead and be top dog if there was to be any chance for law and order to take root in Leantown. If he'd been there, folks would have thought that John was hiding behind Jackson's gun and nothing would have been accomplished.

An hour later, the inevitable happened. A chair was pushed back and a table overturned. An angry red-faced miner was standing facing one of the many gamblers who had made his way to the settlement in hopes of fleecing those who came in search of the heavy metal.

The prospector was drunk and was having a hard time remaining on his feet as he swayed back and forth in front of the gambler whose hand hovered over the .41 caliber Remington derringer in his vest pocket. A derringer wasn't all that effective a weapon when it came to killing a man outright. Usually it was the lint or dirt picked up by the bullet as it entered the body that caused an infection which ended up killing the man who was shot with the small gun. And even though death wasn't immediate—the man still ended up dead in the long run. The main value of a derringer was the threat it implied. Still, at close range and with enough time to take careful aim, the bullet packed enough of a punch to kill if it hit a vital organ; and that was exactly what John figured the gambler was getting ready to do to the blustering prospector as soon as the miner went for his sidearm.

Deciding that it was time to take action, John opened up his coat, exposed the badge and Colt he wore, and moved toward the miner. At the same time he motioned for the nearest deputy to cover the gambler with his double-barreled shotgun.

With the barrels of the Greener staring him in the face, the gambler's hand froze over the derringer, too scared to even move his hand away from the weapon. The prospector, on the other hand, had failed to take notice of that fact and was clawing for his holstered weapon. He had his pistol halfway out of its scabbard by the time Baldwin reached out with his short-barreled Colt to rap him across his temple, causing him to sink to the floor. Disarming the now helpless miner, Ethan stepped around him to remove the gambler's derringer—careful not to walk in front of the deputy wielding the shotgun filled with double-ought buckshot. Seeing that everyone in the saloon was watching every move that he made, John figured that now was the perfect time to introduce himself to the people he would be serving as the town sheriff.

"My name's John Baldwin, and I'm the newly appointed sheriff of Leantown. These men," he said, gesturing at the men wearing badges and toting the shotguns, "are my deputies duly appointed by the mayor and town council members."

"I never heard nothin' 'bout no durn election," said one of the miners well on his way to getting drunk.

"We had our election last night, but only those who had a stake in the community were allowed to vote. We didn't choose to include those of you who are just passing through and will pull up and leave the first time you don't find any color at the bottom of your gold pan. In other words, we only let those vote who planned on being here for awhile.

"And just to make things clear, we intend to run Leantown the same way any civilized community is governed. That means we won't tolerate any killings or robberies—justice will be swift . . . and permanent. So if you value your freedom and your life, I'd advise you to walk easy around town."

It appeared that nobody was inclined to argue the point with Baldwin. Ordinarily several of them would have been inclined to challenge the duded-up sheriff, but they weren't inclined to argue with the hard-eyed deputies packing the double-barreled scatterguns; after all, a little law-and-order wasn't unreasonable. And most of the men in the saloon—while they'd never admit it to each other—were secretly pleased that there was going to be some law in town, for there was a lot to be said to living in a town where a man could go to the sheriff to get justice instead of strapping on a gun to settle matters himself—at least in those towns where the man wearing the badge was honest and not owned by the ones who owned most of the property in the community.

Seeing that the people had accepted his authority, John instructed two of the more sober prospectors to carry the body of the unconscious miner over to the town's makeshift jail with one of his deputies. He then turned back to the bar to enjoy a beer.

At the top of the stairs, staring out the slightly open door he had been hiding behind, Ethan slipped his revolver back into his holster and breathed a sigh of relief. He had been worried about Baldwin and had sneaked into the saloon in anticipation of helping out if necessary. With the crisis having passed, his mind could once again latch onto the letter he'd re-read that evening from his father. It seemed that Cole Jackson—Ethan's kid brother—was becoming more of a handful with each passing day, and Lige Jackson was becoming increasingly concerned that his youngest was headed for trouble.

Chapter Seven
Cole Jackson

Ethan's mind wandered back to the prosperous Jackson farm in central Ohio as he thought of the younger brother who'd only been five years old when he'd packed his grip and headed west many years ago.

Ethan hadn't seen his father or brother for all those many years, the only communication between them being the occasional letter that found Ethan in some lonely outpost or the missive that reached Lige at the post office bearing the postmark from some place with as strange and colorful-sounding a name as the elder Jackson had ever heard during his sixty years of life.

Ethan felt he knew how his father was feeling just then as he was about to lose another offspring to a land of short lives and violent deaths. He also felt he knew how Cole was feeling about being stuck on a farm when he was dying to fork his horse for Texas. And Ethan was right, for Cole was a reluctant seventeen-year-old farmer who was chomping at the bit to saddle the pinto he'd traded a good plowhorse for, stuff his .44 Henry rifle in its scabbard, and ride south to herd cattle in the Lone Star State.

Cole also owned a .44 Schofield handgun, along with a hand-tooled holster and shell-belt he planned to strap on the second he was out of his father's sight. He had to wait until then because he'd been warned by Lige that if he ever heard or saw him wearing the revolver around the farm or town, he'd take it away from him and melt it down in the blacksmith's forge.

Knowing that his father always meant what he said, Cole had been careful not to anger him, and had restricted his fast-draw practicing to the mirror in his bedroom. When practicing his marksmanship, he had always wrapped the weapon in a rag when carrying it to target practice.

Jackson senior had said that Cole could manage to get himself into more than enough trouble with his fists without adding to the expense by having to bail him out of jail for spraying lead all over town; Cole readily agreed with his father on that point. Sometimes it seemed that trouble stuck to him closer than a brother and it was a rare night that didn't find him getting into a fight with some tough in the farming community of Low Ridge, Ohio.

While Cole had yet to use a weapon against any man, he was well-versed in how to use his mitts from having spent many years pounding them against the skulls of those who seemed as prone to getting into disputes as he was himself.

Despite the fact that he lacked practical experience in the use of a handgun, Cole had still managed to get in enough practice with the weapon so that he could draw it swiftly and shoot it accurately. Unfortunately, while his skill with the Schofield had grown, his judgement had been stunted. His father had spent a lot of money to bail his son out of the local jail and to pay for the damages his wayward son's fights had caused around town.

Lige had been determined to keep Cole on the farm

where he could guide his son toward a maturity that would permit him to take his rightful place among his siblings in supervising the many acres controlled by the Jackson family. But due to the death of Cole's best friend in a senselss act of violence, he knew now that the keeping of his son in Ohio might end up getting him killed or hanged.

For many of the people of Low Ridge expected Cole to avenge the death of his well-liked friend—and so did Cole. So far Lige had been able to talk, threaten, and bully his son enough to keep him from going after the man who had killed the preacher's son, but Cole was determined that sooner or later he would be calling on his friend's murderer. And the only way that Lige could think of to keep his son out of trouble was to let him go the way of his older brother. Not that Cole couldn't have defended himself—he could. But because of what would happen later.

The man who had killed Cole's friend was from a large and prominent political family, and if Cole ended up killing him there would be repercussions and vendettas that would rival or beat any of the feuds being fought to the south in Kentucky and West Virginia.

In the end, Lige could see no other solution than to let Cole ride for Texas and try his hand at being a cowboy.

It wasn't easy for Lige to give his blessing to Cole and let him ride off, for while Cole only had some romantic notion about the life of a cowboy, letters from Ethan had let the elder Jackson know what the life of a drover was really like. But even after learning about how a cowboy spent almost all his waking hours in the saddle or how he ended up eating grub a hungry dog would turn its nose up at, Cole refused to give up his romantic notions about cowboying.

Even when his father pointed out the fact that he was eating the best food to be had in the country outside of some fancy big-city restaurant and sleeping in a warm feather bed almost every night, the youngest Jackson would not admit his folly. It was at this point Lige began to wonder if his son had fallen on his head and lost what little sense he had. After all, to go riding off into a situation you hadn't been made aware of was one thing. To leave the comfortable life he enjoyed on the farm to live the life of a vagabond was just something the elder Jackson couldn't comprehend.

But Cole was young and only laughed at his father's praise for the life of a well-to-do farmer. For him, as it had been for Ethan, a life lived on the edge was much preferred to a life spent dreaming of adventure on a comfortable feather bed. So when his father suggested that he give cowboying a try, he jumped at the chance and hoped his father wouldn't change his mind before he could pack.

Riding his pinto away from the farm where he'd been born and had lived for all of his seventeen years caused him to have emotions of regret mixed with his feeling of elation at finally being on his way west. He had no definite plans about where he wanted to go, but since it was winter, Cole figured that a southerly direction was a pretty good place to start. His ultimate goal was to join a trail drive that would more than likely be headed for Kansas. Kansas was the last place he'd heard that Ethan had been working as sheriff—it would be nice to see his older brother again.

First he had to get hired on as a drover with one of the herds being driven north. He figured that Texas would be a good place to start looking for somebody putting a herd together. At the very least he figured the weather would be more moderate, and if he couldn't find work right off, well, there was always Mexico, where he could spend the winter without spending much of his money while waiting for a job.

There was also the small matter of getting justice for his murdered friend. The coroner had ruled that Barney Jules's death had been an accident, but Cole figured that when two men held another man by his arms while a third thug beat him until he lost consciousness and then continued to pummel the helpless victim, it was nothing short of murder. Two of those three men had already paid the ultimate fine for their heinous act—they were dead. But the man who had been behind it, Jeremy Adams, still owed his debt to society as Cole saw it. Unfortunately, Jeremy's father was a prominent Ohio politician who had more than enough money to buy his son out of whatever trouble he might care to get into.

Cole knew why his father had finally given his blessing for him to leave the farm, and he hated to thwart his father's plan to avoid trouble, but this would be his last chance to even the score with Jeremy Adams.

Cole had refrained from bracing Adams in deference to his father's wishes. He knew that Jeremy's father would seek revenge against anyone—lawman or friend of the deceased—who tried to bring his only son to justice. And even if there had been a lawman brave, or foolish, enough to arrest Jeremy, there was no chance of a jury made up of twelve men from the community of Low Ridge convicting the son of a man to whom each and every one of them owed money or a favor. Even if they could find twelve men who didn't owe the rich and powerful Adams, they would have to run the gauntlet formed by the henchmen Andy Adams kept on his payroll to handle the problems the prominent politician couldn't fix with a favor or money.

Even with his limited experience dealing with those wielding political power, Cole understood that there was little chance that the murderer of his friend would ever be brought to trial, and if Barney Jules was going to get justice, it would have to be meted out with the help of "Judge Colt."

There was only one saloon in the community, and it was the place where those prone to taking a drink on occasion tended to congregate. Jeremy Adams was known to go there every night. Adams had taken to carrying a short-barreled Colt in a shoulder rig and was getting to be known for his habit of trying his fast draw on unsuspecting members of the community. He'd even pulled his gun on an unarmed Cole on one occasion.

More than one man, forgetting for the moment whose son he was, had needed to be restrained by the two Pinkerton detectives hired as bodyguards from throttling the young Adams. The two beefy detectives had been shadowing Jeremy ever since word had gotten back to Andy Adams about what had happened to the Jules kid. It was the Pinkertons' job to make certain that no one plugged the beloved only child of Andy Adams—a job that was becoming harder to do with each passing day, for Jeremy was the kind of client that many people would have been happy to shoot.

The senior Adams knew that someone, sooner or later, would try to get revenge for the popular young man that his son had so brutally beaten to death for no other reason than the fact that he could do so and get away with it. His son's actions disgusted even the ruthless Andy Adams. Still, he was blood and a man had to look out for his own kind no matter what. He only hoped that the protection he was paying such a high price for in the form of the two Pinkertons would scare off any would-be assasins and, failing that, he hoped the Pinkertons would prove to be better shots than the assailant who went after his son.

Walking into the saloon that night Cole wasn't surprised to find Jeremy Adams sitting at a table at the back of the room flanked by his two beefy Pinkerton guards. Jeremy also spotted the young Jackson as he strode purposely into the room; he spotted the tied-down gun he was wearing as well. Since he knew that Cole's father had forbidden him to wear the sidearm around town, he figured that Cole must be pretty serious to openly defy the elder Jackson. When he thought that he might be the reason for this defiance, he shuddered.

Sensing trouble and noticing that Ethan was wearing a gun, all of the men who were standing between Jackson and Adams parted, opening up a path between them. The Pinkertons got to their feet and began to lumber toward the seventeen-year-old kid wearing the tied-down gun, but when each of the detectives felt a gun being stuck in his ribs, he suddenly remembered that he didn't like the man he'd been guarding and allowed himself to be pulled to the side. Barney Jules had friends other than Cole Jackson in the community, and they weren't about to allow anybody to get in the way of justice.

Sweat had started to break out on Jeremy's forehead; for the first time in his life he was facing a man without anybody else to help him or hold his opponent still while he pummeled him into a state of unconsciousness. Worse was the fact that this man was also armed; and while Cole had never had a gunfight with anyone, his brother was the infamous Ethan Jackson known for his skill with a gun, and was reported to have bested twenty men in gunfights—so far. Could Cole be as good with a gun as his famous brother? And even if he weren't, was the son of Andy Adams, the politician, good enough to take on even a moderately skilled gunslinger more accustomed to a plow handle than the handle of a Colt? Jeremy really didn't want to find out and wished fervently that he had stayed at home like his father had asked him. But what did he have to worry about—nobody in Low Ridge had the nerve to buck his father's money and power and besides, what was his father paying the two big oxes who shadowed his every move for if he had to stay at home?

Stopping in front of Jeremy's table and hooking his thumbs in front of his gunbelt, Cole said, "I reckon you know why I'm here, Adams."

"Yeah, I know, Jackson," replied Adams, who was trying to appear unconcerned about facing Barney Jules' best friend—by himself. Unfortunately for Jeremy, the sweat forming on his upper lip and the perspiration popping out on his forehead was betraying his true feeling of fear.

"I came here to give you a choice, Jeremy," said Cole.

"Choice?"

"That's right. You can either admit that you murdered Barney Jules," Jackson said as he unhooked the thumb of his right hand from his belt and let it dangle beside his sidearm, "or you can draw that gun you're so fond of pulling on unarmed folks—your choice."

Blinking the sweat from his eyes, Jeremy began to shake as he stared into Cole's eyes. For a second, he could have sworn that he saw the Grim Reaper staring back at him. But as soon as he took notice of the fact that he hadn't sprung any leaks from bullet holes, he calmed down enough to be able to think clearly again. Why not give Jackson the confession he was asking for? He could always change his story later on—say that he was only trying to calm down an enraged man with a gun who was apt to start throwing lead in a crowded saloon if he didn't get what he was asking for. That would look good in court—show that he was the kind of man who thought of other folks' safety. He might even come out of this whole thing looking like some kind of a hero—he liked the idea of that.

"All right, Jackson," he said, spreading his arms on the

table to make it obvious that his hands were nowhere near the gun in his shoulder holster. "Have it your way—I murdered Barney Jules." Then, in an attempt to point out that if Cole now shot him, he would be considered guilty of a crime, he asked, "What are you going to do now—murder *me?*"

Adams was finding it hard not to smile; he had outwitted the pistol-packing farm boy. But if he had been so foolish as to have let a smile cross his lips, it would have instantly disappeared, for Jackson immediately drew his revolver and leveled it at a spot right above Jeremy's nose.

Keeping the Schofield trained on the profusely sweating Adams, Cole walked around the table and lifted Jeremy's short-barreled Colt from its shoulder holster and holstered his own weapon. Breaking open the loading gate of Adams's gun, Cole turned up the Colt and let each shell fall to the floor as he turned the cylinder.

Tossing the now-useless weapon onto the table, Jackson said, "You just confessed to murder, Adams; everybody here already knew you were guilty—I just wanted you to admit it to them. Sooner or later the law will catch up to you and you'll pay for what you did. But I won't kill you. You see, my pa told me a long time ago that it was poor business to kill a coward. Because when it's somebody like you who needs killin', it would mean trading my life for yours by being hanged or spending a good part of my life in prison, over somebody who's not worth spending a night in a county jail."

Turning his back on Adams, Cole began to walk away. Staring at Jackson's back as he walked toward the door, Jeremy knew that what Cole had said had the ring of truth about it. The words he had used stung the proud Jeremy Adams—what would his father have to say; not only about his confession but about the fact that he, an Adams, had backed down from a plow boy and allowed him to slander the family name without so much as calling Jackson a liar.

Staring at the empty gun lying on the table in front of him, Jeremy sorely wished that Cole had neglected to unload the weapon. Then he noticed that the man standing beside him was carrying a handgun stuffed into his waistband. Grabbing the pistol, Adams drew down on Cole's back and fired.

Cole fell to the floor—his life's-blood flowing out of him. Jeremy arrogantly walked up to the fallen Jackson, eared back the hammer on the stolen revolver, and leveled it at Cole's head. A hollow boom sounded in the tightly packed room and black powder smoke dispersed throughout the saloon.

When the smoke cleared Jackson was still alive, but Jeremy Adams lay dead with a bullet hole in the back of his head—one of Barney's friends had avenged him and saved Cole Jackson's life in the process.

It was early morning before Jackson regained consciousness. The bullet that had felled him the night before had entered his back on the left side and exited through his chest, barely missing his heart. Fortunately no arteries or organs had been hit and what damage had been done by the hot metal would heal. Still, the loss of blood caused by the back-shooting Adams's actions would have killed Cole if Doc Emerson hadn't been in town to stop the bleeding.

Two days later, the young Jackson was healthy enough to be moved to the farm where he could recuperate under the supervision of his father, who would no doubt have plenty to say about Cole's lack of judgement, and might even melt down his Schofield in the forge as he had promised. Still, Cole looked forward to getting home. Just as he was getting ready to go downstairs to the waiting buckboard that would take him to the Jackson farm, however, the sheriff showed up at Emerson's office with a warrant for his arrest for the murder of Jeremy Adams.

It seemed that since no one could be found to blame the shooting itself on, Andy Adams, determined to avenge his son's killing, was charging Cole with causing Jeremy's death through his actions in the saloon that night. He had badgered the prosecutor into charging Jackson with murder, just as he had badgered him into calling Barney Jules's death an accident.

If the politically prominent Adams had his way, he would see to it that Cole Jackson was swinging at the end of a rope before Christmas—and Andy Adams always got his way.

Lige Jackson headed for town as soon as the buckboard returned to the farm without his son. He wore a look of deep concern etched on his weathered face as he spoke to his son through the bars of his cell. "Well, you sure stepped into it this time, son," he said as he leaned forward in the straight back chair outside the cell.

"I guess so, Pa. But I never fired a shot in the saloon that night and there's a room full of witnesses who can swear to that—including those two Pinkertons who were guarding Jeremy that night. I don't see how they could convict me of murder."

"Oh, they can all right," assured the elder Jackson. "You'd be surprised. . . . I should say you *will* be surprised what money and a good lawyer can get done in a court of law."

"Speaking of that," said Cole, "what exactly is it that they are trying to get done?"

Looking somewhat disgusted at his son's lack of perception, Lige said, "Why, they're fixin' to try and hang you. Haven't you caught on to that yet?" The elder Jackson wondered if his son had bumped his head on something when he was shot.

"Oh, I understand that Pa, what I meant was how are they planning on charging me with murder when I didn't shoot him and he was the one who shot me in the back—and from what I've been told would have finished me off if someone hadn't done for him in time to save my hide. It just don't make sense to me."

"Son, the law don't have to make sense—it's the law. But to answer your question, Adams is claiming that your little stunt in the saloon that night resulted in his son's death, and as such, you are just as guilty of murder as the man who pulled the trigger."

Cole knew he was in bad trouble and that his father wouldn't appreciate what he was about to say, but he couldn't help saying it anyway. "We don't have a thing to worry about, Pa," said Cole, smiling.

"How you figure that?" asked his worried father.

"Why, as soon as our sharp-as-a-tack coroner spots the bullet hole in the back of Jeremy Adams's head, he'll rule it an accidental shooting. We don't have a thing to worry about in the world." Cole leaned back on his bed and laughed.

Lige's face turned three different shades of red as his blood began to boil, and he reached for his son's throat behind the bars. Cole, despite the seriousness of his wound, was still quick enough to avoid his father's grasp.

Forcing himself to calm down, Lige said, "Boy, you sure are a trial. I don't know how it is that any lawyer is going to be able to tolerate your behavior long enough to defend your sorry hide—if I can find one, that is."

"What do you mean by that, Pa?"

"It means that no lawyer in town will take your case because of Andy Adams—they're afraid of what he could do to them politically. And they're afraid of the hired thugs he keeps on his payroll. I've had to send word out of state to find an attorney for you; and if one is dumb enough to take on the job, I'll have to be hiring bodyguards to watch over him during your trial. Like I said before, you've really stepped into it this time."

Cole thought of telling his father where he could find two out-of-work Pinkertons to act as guards for the attorney, but he didn't feel quite up to dodging another attack by his enraged parent. Besides, the two Pinks weren't all that great at their jobs when you got right down to it.

The days before Cole's trial dragged by; especially since he'd been denied bail for fear he might decide to run rather than go to trial. Not that Cole could blame them for that. If let outside of the jail, the sight of a saddled horse might be all of the incentive he needed to "rabbit." So he remained in jail during the cold November days that seemed to never end.

Finally, on December 3, Cole found himself on the Low Ridge courthouse steps getting ready to stand trial for the murder of Jeremy Adams. In attendance were Lige Jackson, Andy Adams and his henchmen, and the county prosecutor, Silas Martin, who, with the sudden illness of the regular county attorney requiring the appointment of another lawyer to the post, just happened to be the best lawyer in the state of Ohio. On Jackson's side there was his attorney, Isaac Tolliver, the only person from out of state in attendance, and every citizen of Low Ridge, Ohio who could be packed within the confines of the courtroom.

Presiding over the trial was Judge Moses Franklin—a jurist who owed Adams many a favor, but who was also aware of the sentiment in the community concerning what Andy Adams's son had done. He was also well aware of the fact that Lige Jackson had money that could be used against him during upcoming elections if he showed too much partiality towards the prosecution. Franklin had decided to be very cautious about how he conducted himself during the trial. Given the tight-rope he was going to have to walk between Adams and Jackson, he was as nervous as a long-tailed cat in a room full of rocking chairs.

Tolliver was the only ally Jackson had in the battle that was about to take place. Tolliver had a reputation as a fiery lawyer from eastern Kentucky, who Cole thought of as something of a cross between a circuit-riding preacher and, because of his small stature and a shock of red hair atop his head, a banty rooster.

When Cole had looked at his father questioningly after meeting Tolliver, Lige knew what he was thinking. He told him that the Kentucky lawyer was the only man he could find with enough nerve—or desperate enough for a fee— to take on the job of defending him. Cole began to wonder how painful hanging by the neck was when it came to forms of execution, and whether or not he should ask to be shot instead. Things didn't look so good as far as he was concerned.

Judge Franklin called the court to order and Cole, who knew that Franklin owed Adams for contributions to his campaign and other favors, offered up a silent prayer that he would still be fair during the trial.

Silas Martin led off the proceeding with a fiery speech that extolled the virtues of young Jeremy Adams. By the time the lawyer was finished, Jeremy Adams—to anyone who hadn't known the thug—would have been thought a prime candidate for sainthood who had been cut down much too soon by the ill-advised actions of one Cole Jackson. For those who knew him, they wondered who had given Martin the idea that Adams was such a fine upstanding citizen. Some of those in attendance laughed out loud during the flowery speech, and more than one was heard to ask who the lawyer was talking about and that they had heard *Jeremy Adams* had been shot—not the man the lawyer was describing. Andy Adams's face colored a bright red but he kept looking forward while the prosecutor continued to praise a man whose only virtue was the fact that he would make good worm food—maybe.

Then a parade of witnesses took the stand. It was a one-sided affair, with all of the witnesses friendly to the prosecution. Several of the men who had been present in the saloon that night had been asked to be a witness for the defense but they had declined, not wanting to anger Adams.

Each witness who appeared said the same thing as the one before him. Each claimed that Cole had drawn on Jeremy and threatened him and that young Adams had been afraid for his life and that was why Jeremy had shot Cole. But when asked during cross-examination about Cole saying he wasn't going to kill Jeremy and Cole having his back turned to him when Adams shot him, none of them could remember Cole's words or recall seeing Jeremy shooting him in the back.

At one point, Tolliver became so frustrated with the witnesses' refusal to acknowlege the fact that his client had been shot in the back by the prosecution's purported saint that he had Cole stand and raise his shirt to show the wound, causing an uproar in the courtroom which Franklin had a hard time gaveling down.

When the witnesses were asked about why a saint such as Jeremy Adams would be shot in the back of the head, each witness opined that somebody had probably been taking a shot at Jackson and hit Adams by mistake and he was probably too ashamed to admit that he had accidentally killed the popular young Adams.

Cole noticed that there was something very similar about

those who took the stand that morning: all of them were the dregs of the community who spent most of their time in jail or the saloon—though he couldn't remember any of them being in the saloon the night Jeremy was shot.

Apparently, while the good citizens of the county were afraid of Adams, they were more afraid of putting their hands on a Bible and swearing to a lie. Cole figured that some of them just didn't want their neighbors to remember that they could lie in a court of law. Their neighbors would remember that fact later on when they had dealings with them and act accordingly—it could end up costing them money in the long run. So Adams's lawyer had been reduced to getting his witnesses from the bottom of the barrel.

Isaac Tolliver's reaction to what Cole told him was to request the sheriff's records from the night of the shooting which he perused while court was dismissed for the midday meal. When Tolliver walked into the courtroom that afternoon, he had a spring in his step and a smile on his lips—a smile that caused the prosecutor to go to his notes to review that morning's testimony.

When the session began, the courtroom was so tightly packed that, despite the November weather, it was warm inside. It was Tolliver's turn to cross-examine the last witness—Luther Hanks, the county drunk. He was much too ambitious in his pursuit of corn whiskey to be classified as a mere town drunk. But for someone whose brain stayed in pretty much of a stupor because of John Barleycorn, he showed a remarkable clarity of thought when describing the events that took place in the saloon the night of the shooting. It was almost as if someone had written a speech for him to memorize. In fact, he remembered everything that had happened that night with such precision that his testimony coincided perfectly with what the previous witnesses for the prosecution had said.

Tolliver began his cross-examination by reviewing what Hanks had previously said so it would be fresh in everyone's memory. Then he asked, "And who shot Jeremy Adams?"

Since Tolliver had asked him a question he hadn't been rehearsed in how to answer, Luther took his time in answering. Finally, he replied, "Didn't see who it was."

"Really, Mr. Hanks, I find it hard to believe that a man blessed with your powers of visual perception was unable to see who shot Jeremy Adams."

"What?" asked Hanks, in confusion. "What powers you talkin' 'bout?"

"What I'm referring to is that, according to the sheriff's ledger I've just examined, you and every other witness who has testified here this morning was incarcerated in the county jail at the time of the shooting. And since you and your fellow witnesses could see what happened five hundred feet away from behind locked jail cells and a brick wall, I can only assume that you and your friends are endowed with uncanny powers of sight and that such powers must extend to being able to determine who shot Jeremy Adams."

After a brief stunned silence, laughter erupted, and then applause that completely drowned out the judge's rapidly banging gavel and the prosecutor's shouted objections.

When the noise finally died down to where Franklin's gavel could be heard, Tolliver asked that Hanks and the previous witnesses be held until they could be questioned about their amazing powers of observation.

The judge, who well knew what had happened, looked over at a red-faced Andy Adams, who could only shrug his shoulders in feigned innocence.

Seeing his way out of a very sticky situation, Franklin looked at Tolliver and said, "Case dismissed for lack of evidence. No trial, no perjury; everybody is free to go."

Cheers erupted that could be heard all over town—if anyone had been there to hear them, for almost everyone was in the courthouse at the time. Justice had been done—sort of—and the people were celebrating the fact that an innocent man had been aquitted, despite the fact that the deck had been stacked against him. And the people were able to forget about Andy Adams for awhile and just enjoy themselves.

Adams, however, was in his own little world, ignoring those who were celebrating. He was thinking of ways other than the law that he could use to get the vengeance he craved.

Chapter Eight
Law and Order

John Baldwin was blissfully unaware that the barrel of a Winchester .44–.40 was being pointed at the back of his head and that the slack on the trigger was slowly being taken up by a pudgy trigger finger. Soon the hammer would fall, causing a 200-grain lead projectile to go spinning toward his skull that would end his short career as a lawman forever.

When the hollow boom sounded in the room, it caused everybody—including those who were drunk, or well on their way to getting there—to jerk to attention and spin their heads to the right, where they witnessed a pear-shaped body tumbling down the staircase to the bottom step, where he was easily identified as one Alphonse Wright—owner and proprietor of the Gold Star Saloon. On the side of his head a large lump was starting to form where he'd obviously been struck with something very hard; beside him lay the rifle that had been pointing at Baldwin's head a few seconds earlier—smoke still curling out of the end of the barrel.

Curious, Collins stepped unnoticed to the bat-wing doors

and glanced toward an upstairs window of the saloon, where he saw a familiar form step out onto the ledge, drop to the ground, and quickly disappear up the alley. Muttering under his breath, Jake said, "I didn't figure you'd be able to stay out of it no matter what you told everybody else, Ethan." Then, with a smile on his face, he turned his attention back to Wright, who was being carried out of his establishment to keep company with the drunken miner who had been arrested earlier that evening and who was now enjoying the hospitality of Leantown's makeshift jail.

With two of the more violent denizens of the saloon already residing in the town's new calaboose, the other patrons of the establishment chose to remain peaceful; after all, it did seem to be the prudent thing to do with Baldwin's shotgun-toting deputies scowling at everyone and seeming more than ready to draw down on anybody who so much as even looked like he wanted to cause trouble. The law had come to Leantown.

With peace established, Jake figured it was a good time to check on the party of "Missouri mules" who had tried the snowed-in mountain pass and see if there was anybody left alive to bring back to town.

A week later a bedraggled bunch of sorry tenderfeet straggled back into town with Jake at the lead. Ethan was amazed to find that many of them still had their haughty attitude and wouldn't admit that they had been wrong to try to get over the pass after they were told by those who knew better that such a venture was foolhardy. But at least none of them were talking about trying it again anytime soon. "At least that shows they can learn," Ethan said to Jake soon after he arrived with them in tow.

"They don't seem able to learn all that much to me, and they sure don't learn all that fast," countered Jake.

After that night in the saloon, open disrespect for the

ordinary citizen of Leantown was pretty much over, with only the newcomers to the settlement occasionally bucking the law. Depending on who those newcomers irked on their arrival, they were either warned about Baldwin and his deputies or left to find out on their own about them. For those who ran afoul of the law, their stay could be quite unpleasant.

All things considered, Ethan figured those running the town had developed a pretty fair and efficient form of justice. They were getting along quite well by using their common sense, without relying on the expertise of lawyers and politicians to tell them how things should be run. He thought of it as a good example of what could be done when folks got together with the intention of doing the right thing.

Because of the peace brought about by the new law and order, the citizens of Leantown—the good and the bad—could go about their business and even engage in social activities without fear of being harassed by the rowdier element. And with the weather starting to turn bad, as winter's icy fingers began to wrap around the community's throat, the mines became inactive. People began to congregate to pass the time together and engage in social activities to a much greater extent than they had while searching for the mother lode. Even the dour and sullen semi-permanent residents of the Gold Star Saloon found themselves coming together to participate in poker games and the like. Not only were the private games among friends being kept honest, but also those games of chance run by the house, for Alphonse had been told that he could either run his games honestly or be run out of town on a rail. Rubbing the still-swollen bump on his head, Wright readily agreed to run honest games and had done so ever since.

While Jake readily participated in the games at the saloon, Ethan preferred to spend most of his free time at Sharon O'Brien's store with Sharon and her son Corey, for Corey reminded him very much of his younger brother Cole. And the fact that the young boy looked up to him as some sort of a hero didn't hurt when it came to getting along with him. Ethan had even taken him along on hunting trips with Jake or Kenton and had found him to be alert and quick to notice the habits of wild game. He also had a habit that was rare for young boys his age—he knew when to ask questions and when to keep quiet.

What Ethan liked most about the boy, however, was his ability to take things in stride without falling to pieces when trouble came—a characteristic shared by many brought up on the frontier.

Spending time with Sharon and Corey made Ethan yearn for a life that was peaceful and settled. He visualized working hard at a job during the day and coming home to a family at night where he would sit by the fireplace listening to them tell how their day had gone. But each time he would allow himself to dream of that kind of a life, visions of all the times he'd had a peaceful evening shattered by some fool calling him out into the street to prove his skill with a Colt would come to him. And then he would re-member all the sleepless nights and cold sweats he woke with after each fight where he ended up gunning down an-other reputation-hunting fool.

He knew in his heart that he'd never be able to live the peaceful kind of life he yearned for as long as men strapped on a gun as easily as they put on their pants in the morning. It didn't matter where he went. His reputation would follow him—Jake had been right about that. And what would hap-pen to Sharon and Corey? He knew the answer to that also—they'd always be in the line of fire as long as he was around them.

Jackson knew that for the benefit of the two people he was beginning to care so deeply about, he should pack up and leave. While his head told him that was the best and smartest thing to do, though, his heart wouldn't allow it to happen. So while he knew he should be sending Jake to the store to buy what they needed and letting him and Kenton take on the job of teaching the boy about how to survive and thrive in the wilderness, he continued to spend all his free time with the O'Briens and push his dark thoughts about what was bound to happen to the side.

Then there was the problem of the town itself, for while it was growing and prospering because of the gold, it was only a matter of time before the gold would run out and with it would go most of the people living in Leantown. Even if Ethan led them to where he made the strike in the Big Horn Mountains, the gold would eventually run out there too. There was just no getting around the fact that without some form of enterprise, Leantown would dry up and blow away eventually.

While Ethan knew he should have been making plans to leave himself, he found himself staying on and growing more fond of Sharon and Corey with each passing day. But even in his courtship of Sharon he found he did not have a clear path, for her other suitors were both numerous and persistent. Many of them made no secret of the fact that they intended to muscle the ex-lawman completely out of the picture, although none of them were inclined to confront him face-to-face concerning the matter, preferring to show up on her doorstep only when Ethan wasn't around.

Given the fact that there were so few eligible females in the mostly male mining community, there was usually at least one fight a day breaking out among those who were competing for the lovely and very wealthy Sharon O'Brien's hand, with even those too old to be interested in romance throwing their hats into the matrimonial ring in hopes of being chosen by her to manage her increasingly profitable assets.

But these men lacked ardor, and except for the money that was to be gained by signing a marriage contract, there was very little they had passion for. This resulted in their rivalries—for the most part—being non-violent. Unfortunately, there were plenty of men around who *were* passionate and who were more than willing to let any dispute they might find themselves in be settled with guns, knives, or fists. It was this type of suitor who kept Baldwin and his deputies busy breaking up fights at Sharon's store and restaurant on a regular basis—at least when Ethan wasn't hanging around those establishments.

On one occasion John had become so frustrated that he told Ethan he wished that he'd marry the O'Brien woman so he and his deputies could do something other than spend most of their time breaking up fights among her admirers.

Baldwin had been joking, but there was no denying that there was more than a kernel of truth in what he'd said. Just last Thursday afternoon, as Ethan was hanging around the store, three suitors strode through the door. When they saw Jackson inside, they all quickly turned and left—the last one slamming the door and leaving in a huff to express his displeasure at finding him there.

"Well, looks like I just lost you another suitor," Ethan said.

Sighing, Sharon said, "No need to worry about that, there'll be another one showing up within an hour. They're peskier than flies in July when you're trying to butcher a chicken."

"Sure seems that way," agreed Jackson.

"It wouldn't be so bad if they didn't get in my way while I was trying to wait on my real customers. Sometimes, when you're not around, they show up early in the morning and just hang around all day until another one of them shows up and a fight breaks out. I just wish there were some more single women in town—I could use the peace and quiet," Sharon said.

Corey, who was stocking the shelves, said, "There are other single women in town, Ma. I've seen them over at the saloon. But they wear funny-looking clothes and put some sort of paint on their faces."

Sharon O'Brien's face turned a bright red as she said, "Hush now, Corey, and you make sure that you stay away from that saloon."

"Why, Ma?"

"Just never you mind, young man, you just do what I say."

Ethan was chuckling at Sharon's embarrassment. "But none of them are as pretty as your ma, are they, Corey?" asked Ethan.

"Oh, no sir! Ma's the prettiest girl in town all right," replied Corey.

The beautiful storekeeper's blush turned a darker shade of red from the compliment and she said, "Corey, why don't you go outside and check up on the warehouse. Make sure that the patching we did yesterday to keep the varmints out did what it was supposed to do."

"Sure, Ma."

Sharon had hoped that by sending her son outside to do something else he would get sidetracked and not ask any more embarrassing questions. But Mrs. O'Brien wasn't about to get her wish, for when Corey reached the door he turned around, faced Ethan, and said, "You know, Mr. Jackson, if you was to marry Ma other men wouldn't be coming around here getting into fights." Without waiting for a reply, Corey turned and ran out the door toward the storehouse to do as he had been told.

Sharon was beginning to think that her face might stay permanently red—or at the very least, catch on fire—or possibly she might just die of embarrassment. Even Ethan was beginning to feel downright uncomfortable. Jackson had never ceased to be amazed at how quickly a child could get to the heart of a matter by stating the obvious while all of the adults involved in the situation would hem and haw all around the simple truth.

Then a voice came from Ethan he almost didn't seem aware of. "He's right, you know."

Sharon reached out to the wall to steady herself before she asked, "Right about what?"

"Corey's right about me marrying you and all. My marrying you would stop the suitors and let you live in peace," said Jackson.

Sharon was surprised, and then tears began to form in her eyes, for Ethan was the only man she had been interested in, and now he was saying he was serious about her. Moving to each other they embraced and kissed—a kiss that lasted until a smiling Corey bounded into the store with the news that the chinking they had fixed the store with had held. It was good news, but even at just ten years of age, Corey could tell that what he had interrupted between his mother and Ethan Jackson was even better news. It was going to be nice to have a full-time father again.

Later, Jackson would reflect on how what he had said that afternoon would affect his life; more importantly, he would also begin to think about how his actions would affect Sharon and Corey's lives as well. Then there was the consideration about how and where they would live. For, sooner or later, most of the gold would be mined out of the area and Leantown would go back to being what it once was—a dying community.

Once again, Ethan reminded himself that Leantown lacked an industry that would allow it to grow and prosper; or, for that matter, survive. With the prospect of taking on the added responsibility of a wife and a son, the idea of their home becoming worthless was something Jackson was finding hard to admit even to himself. Then there was the fact that he was living in a community of people most of whom he personally liked. That gave him a feeling of belonging somewhere he hadn't known since he'd left Low Ridge, Ohio. He despised the idea of leaving a place where he could bring up his family among friends. With that thought in his mind, he spent most of the night trying to think of ways that Leantown could survive; it was a shame that gold couldn't be replenished like crops.

The next morning, Ethan, Caleb Kenton, and Corey decided to take advantage of the break in the weather and do some hunting in hopes of adding some fresh venison—maybe even some tasty elk steaks—to the restaurant's menu. Corey also wanted to get a chance to harvest his first big game animal that day. He was hoping to get a shot at an elk, but a mule deer would make him almost as happy. Ethan planned on doing everything in his power that day to see to it that young Corey got his wish—after all, it was his birthday.

Riding through the snow drifts was a pretty tough job with Kenton and Jackson taking turns breaking trail so as to keep from wearing out one horse completely. After an hour and a half of plodding through the drifts they came upon another valley, this one even wider and more sheltered than the one in which Leantown was located. Kenton and Jackson marveled at the scenery. There were plenty of trees, water, and lots of open flat ground where they were sure wild game would abound—a sort of frozen garden of Eden. Ethan had no doubt that on such an unseasonably warm day as they were experiencing, wild game was certain to be out and about. Corey had a very good chance of downing a wapiti.

As he rode down into the valley, a seed of an idea began to germinate in Ethan's brain. It was a seed that had been planted the instant he laid eyes on the valley, so as he scanned the sheltered area for game he was also thinking about the idea that had taken root in his mind. With his mind thus occupied, it wasn't surprising that Kenton was the first one of them to spot the bull elk ghosting through the trees below them.

Dismounting, Ethan and Corey quickly but quietly began to work their way in the direction the elk was traveling in hopes of ambushing the big animal. It was hard work but they finally reached a spot where they set up an ambush, with Corey resting the barrel of the .44–.40 Winchester on a snowdrift he was hiding behind.

Finally the elk walked out into the open, where young O'Brien lined up the sights of the rifle where the back of the right foreleg intersected the elk's chest, just as he had been told to do countless times before.

The barrel of the rifle jumped into the air and its stock pushed against Corey's shoulder. At the edge of the billowing smoke he could see the elk running back to the cover of the trees. Jacking another shell into the rifle's chamber, Corey led the animal with the front sight of the weapon as he had been taught and had begun to take up slack on the trigger when Jackson laid a hand on his shoulder and said, "Don't waste the bullet. It was a good hit; the bull will go down soon."

Then, as if to verify what Ethan had said, there was a loud crash in the woods as the bull elk fell to the ground.

Taking their time, Ethan and Corey followed the blood trail until they found the elk piled up at the edge of a deadfall. Kenton, who had brought the horses into the valley after he had heard the shot, joined Ethan in slapping O'Brien's back and congratulating him on his first big game animal. And it was definitely a big game animal. Caleb guessed that it weighed close to 1500 pounds. It was quite an accomplishment during that time of the year for anyone—man or boy—to put that much meat on the table.

Leaving the more skilled Kenton to teach the boy about the best way to field dress such a large animal, Ethan took off to do some more exploring. Anybody who had seen him then would have thought that he was spying out some likely areas to hunt for gold. But he wasn't thinking about gold just then; he was thinking of a way to make money that would last much longer than a transitory mining venture. As he walked around the rim of the valley he noticed that there were hundreds of unclaimed acres running for several miles—they would be perfect for what he had in mind. He needed help . . . and partners if he was going to save the town.

Wyoming winters were expected to be harsh, and the winter of 1877 lived up to the territory's reputation for being cruel. So when spring finally arrived, there was a frenzy among the miners and the townspeople to make up for lost time. Even Ethan wasn't immune to the idea of getting rich, so as soon as things started to "green up," he rode back to the valley to make sure that it was what he thought it would be as soon as the grass started to sprout— it was. He would speak with Kenton that night and tell Sharon and Corey that he would have to leave Leantown for several months, but if things worked out as he hoped they would, all of their futures would be assured.

Riding back into town that afternoon Jackson noticed that a crowd had gathered around the general store. Dismounting, Ethan walked over to where Corey was standing.

"What's going on?" Ethan asked.

Seeing Ethan beside him, Corey gave up his battle to control his emotions and began to sob uncontrollably. Knowing that something horrible must have happened to make an eleven-year-old boy abandon his carefully hoarded stock of toughness, Jackson began to tremble. He thought of all the possible things that could have happened to make someone as tough as Corey cry in public the way he was now doing. The only thing he could think of was that something must have happened to Sharon. Kneeling down until he was eye level with the young boy, he asked, "What's wrong, Corey?"

Corey tried to tell him, but all he could get out was, "Ma . . . inside."

Leaving Corey at the bottom of the steps, Ethan made his way to the front of the building where Jake was standing. Without being asked, Jake began to fill him in on what had taken place. "Three new arrivals came into the store this morning and tried to have their way with Sharon, but two of Baldwin's deputies were close by as usual and they stopped 'em."

"What happened then?"

"One of the deputies got killed in the gunfight that followed and the other one got shot up pretty bad—seems that the men who done the shootin' are professional gunfighters. Baldwin's up front there waiting for his night deputy to show up so they can rush the door and shoot it out with 'em."

"That's not a real good plan if they figure on keeping Sharon alive," Jackson said.

"I know, but so far nobody has come up with any other ideas," replied Jake.

Stepping back, Jackson glanced across the street and spotted a window that was in line with the storeroom.

"You still got that old buffalo gun?" asked Ethan.

"Yep."

"Can you still hit a gnat at a hundred yards with it?"

"Anytime I need to," replied the mountain man.

"Good. Take up a position over there," he said, pointing at the window, "and after I'm inside and you see your chance, cut down the odds against me as much as you can."

Nodding, Jake took off at a trot to retrieve his weapon and take up his position across the street.

Walking to the door where John was waiting, Ethan said, "Understand that you're planning on rushing in there as soon as your deputy gets here."

"I know it's not much of a plan, but it was the only thing I could think of at the time."

Looking Baldwin in the eye, Jackson asked, "You willing to take another lesson from an old lawman?"

The relief showing on his face, John answered, "Always."

"All right," said Jackson as he took the thong off of his Colt, opened the loading gate, and dropped a sixth cartridge into the cylinder.

"I thought you told me never to let the hammer rest on a live shell," Baldwin said.

"I did, but that was for general carry. When you're about to face three gunslingers with nothing to lose, you want all of the firepower you can get your hands on. And I've found that it's not a real good idea to stop in the middle of a gunfight to reload—most gunmen just ain't all that considerate when it comes to letting a man do something like that."

"What's your plan?" Baldwin asked.

"First, hand me the cane."

Baldwin did so, then took the holster and shell belt from his friend as he handed it over to him; Ethan had stuck his .45 into the waistband of his pants.

"I'm walking in there like I'm drunk. And if things work out like I hope, Jake will take out one of the gunmen from across the street with his rifle, I'll get one of them, and hopefully you'll be able to get in there in time to get the last one."

Rumpling his clothes in an attempt to appear disheveled, Ethan said, "Get your gun out and wait for the first shot." Using the cane to support a supposedly damaged leg, Jackson hoped that the gunmen would think he was crippled and unarmed—it was an edge he desperately needed.

Staggering into the room, Ethan began to wave the cane about while shouting, "Sharon! Sharon! Dad blast it woman where you hidin' at? I'm a needin' some 'backer' and I ain't got all day to waste a gettin' it either."

The first inclination of the three men inside of the store was to start shooting at Jackson the second he stepped inside the store, but they were professional gunmen who weren't inclined to waste lead on someone who didn't appear to be much of a threat. Through his years of wearing a badge, Ethan had found it useful to engage in a bit of playacting on occasion, as he was doing at the moment.

"Store's closed, you blasted drunk, get lost," said the gunman standing closest to the terrified Sharon O'Brien.

Pointing the cane at a tin of tobacco on the top shelf, Ethan said, "That's what I came in here for."

Moving from behind the counter with the intention of throwing the annoying drunk out of the store, one of the gunslingers only walked three feet before a good part of his head exploded from the slug of a .45–.70 Sharps buffalo gun entering his right temple.

The remaining killers were confused, which gave Ethan the opportunity to use the cane like it was a pool cue and jab it into the nearest man's stomach, then swing it like a club to smash its heavy silver handle against his skull. The third gunhand was too far away for Jackson to use the cane against and he had already drawn his gun and was pointing the cocked weapon at Ethan. It was a desperate situation, but Ethan had never been the type of man to give up. Knifing his hand backwards, Jackson pulled back the skirt of his coat to expose the ivory-handled grip of the Colt in his waistband and begin his draw, but the third man already had his pistol out and had begun to gently squeeze the trigger. Jackson was fast but there was no way he could draw and fire before his opponent dropped the hammer.

Figuring that his time was up, Ethan hoped that Sharon would survive. Suddenly he noticed that the third gunman was firing his weapon into the plank floor and toppling over as blood began to seep through his shirt.

Glancing to his left, Ethan saw John Baldwin holding his smoking Colt out in front of him—the weapon that he had taught the lawman how to shoot! He silently congratulated himself for making such a wise investment of his time.

Cutting the ropes binding Sharon, they embraced and Sharon said, "They came in here looking for a Jackson."

Ethan grimaced as he said, "I told you what would happen. It's just happening earlier than I expected."

"No. You don't understand. The Jackson they were hunting for was Cole Jackson—your brother."

Chapter Nine
Trail Hand

Cole was on his third week of riding for an outfit pushing a herd of two thousand steers toward Dodge City, Kansas. He no longer needed to have his father reading him Ethan's descriptions of what cowboy life was really like—he now had firsthand knowlege about how a cowboy lived on the trail. It was an education that Cole wished he had never sought, and as soon as he reached Dodge City he planned to find some other way to make a living.

At that point in his life he would have been more than happy to return to his feather bed in Low Ridge, Ohio; but life there had not only become uncomfortable for him, but downright dangerous as well. It wasn't just him feeling the wrath of Andy Adams, but his entire family and their farmhands as well. His father was losing contracts with old customers on an almost daily basis because of Adams's connections, while his hands were turning up shot or hurt in mysterious accidents around town or on the farm.

The elder Jackson wasn't the type of man to give in to pressure and threats of violence, however. He had tried to keep things peaceful in the small farming community, but when it became clear that Adams was determined that someone—preferably Cole Jackson—was going to pay for the death of his son, Cole's father dug in his heels and got ready to fight Adams if it took everything he owned and the last drop of his blood.

Cole knew that neither of those two men would ever give in and that the only way that peace would return to his family's small section of Ohio would be when he died or, possibly, when he left the state.

Deciding that it was best for all involved for him to disappear, Cole rode away from his childhood home under the cover of darkness one cold and wet February night. Young Jackson had been right in thinking that with his departure the attacks against his father's business and assaults against their hands would halt. But Adams was much too stubborn and filled with grief and hate to stop his pursuit of Cole. So Jackson wasn't surprised when he had his first run-in with one of Andy Adams's hired killers in Texas.

Cole had no experience as a gunhand, and if the hired killer hadn't had the misfortune of having his gun hang up in his new, unbroken-in holster, Cole's body would be resting in some Texas graveyard. But luck had been with the youngest Jackson that night, depending on how one looked at it, and he had ended up killing his first man. It was also that night that Cole learned Andy Adams had hired Morgan Hawks—a well known gun-for-hire—to see to it that Cole never enjoyed another birthday. The dying killer had told his intended victim about Hawks in the spirit of atonement and in hopes that it might pay a small portion of the debt he had run up during a life spent mostly killing folks.

So there it was. Morgan Hawks wasn't the kind of man to restrict his killing to murders that he himself would commit, but would be quite happy to contract out any killings he might not be interested in doing himself. And with the well-to-do Adams footing the bill, Cole knew that he could expect to run into plenty more of the gun-for-hire types known to frequent the more lawless parts of the country.

Having recently turned eighteen, Cole began to reflect on how wrong he had been concerning his wish to be a cowboy. Considering the fact that Adams had put a price on his head, he also began to wonder about just how short his life could end up being.

The men he shared a campfire with at night and worked cattle with during the day didn't make his life any easier or happier. They certainly didn't fit the description that Jackson had dreamed up about how a cowboy looked and acted. Some of them were so young that if he had described them as wet behind the ears, he would have been giving them credit for a couple of years they hadn't lived yet. The older men were what one could have described as ancient. A couple of them were just a couple of years from having to be helped up on their horses.

The ones who were closest to Cole's age weren't what anyone would describe as being overburdened with brains, and a couple of them could only be described as downright mean, especially the nineteen-year-old Cork Jones, who told people that he was called Cork because of his fondness for drinking—as in being known to pull a cork. The real story behind the nickname was that when he was a kid and had been out in the sun for a long time his skin turned brown. Coupled with the fact that his skin was so badly pockmarked, somebody made the comment that with his short body and appearance, he looked for all the world like a cork sticking in the top of a bottle of whiskey. The name just stuck, and since he couldn't do anything to change the unwanted name, he decided to change the story about how he came to be saddled with it.

Cork was the type of kid, and now man, who took a great deal of pleasure in torturing and harassing folks who couldn't or wouldn't fight back. Despite the fact that he had started out as someone of small stature, he had grown to be over six feet tall and weighed round two hundred and fifty pounds. What made him really dangerous, though, was the fact that he had begun to think of himself as something of a gunslinger. But that was only because of the fact that he had stayed in the small town in which he was born and had never seen a real gunman in action. Since most of the population of his hometown were old men who were too tired and old to move on or really do much of anything, he had mistaked his youth for a mark of superiority and had been cutting a wide swath through the community.

But Jones had made even the tired old men in town angry with his boastful posturing. One night, after getting drunk, Cork struck an old man who had been walking with a cane down the town's main street. Three days later, a committee made up of the town's longtime residents visited Cork and explained to him about how healthy other parts of the state might be for a man like him to move to, and how unhealthy it might turn out to be for somebody like him in their peaceful little town.

Jones took a long hard look at the men who were facing him and for the first time realized that the men he had always thought of as being just old and cowardly had been tolerating the loudmouthed behavior of a kid who had taken to wearing a tied-down gun and strutting around town. If Cork had ever bothered to ask about the people who made up his sleepy little Texas town he would have found out that many of them had been in the military. Those who hadn't served some army had stood with their wives and children and fought the Kiowa, Comanches, and Comancheros to a standstill many times. When left alone to go their own way, Cork's neighbors were a generous, understanding people. If pushed, they could turn mean at the drop of a hat—and Jones had just dropped the hat as far as they were concerned.

The next day, Cork packed his belongings, saddled his horse, and rode away from his parent's ranch. He'd learned that it was a bad idea to mess with people who you really didn't know. Perhaps if his visitors that day had demonstrated their displeasure with his behavior, Jones wouldn't have been so quick to fall back into his old habits of bullying other folks. It was also unfortunate that he found a very good place to take up his old habits when he signed on with the cattle drive.

Because of his previous experience, Cork was slow to pick on the older men, but he rarely missed a chance to harass those his own age or younger. The only one he hadn't tried was Cole Jackson; there was just something about him that made Jones wary. Maybe it was the fact that he was the brother of the infamous Ethan Jackson, but Cork didn't think that was the reason. There was just something about Cole that made Cork really nervous. But Jones's nature wouldn't allow him to leave well enough alone—he just had to push Cole sooner or later to see what would happen.

The man who owned the herd was named Zachariah Plott; he was also acting as trail boss on the drive. Plott was a careful and deliberate man of about forty years of age who had tied up almost every penny he had in the world in the drive and wasn't about to tolerate any drinking, fighting, or gunplay that might cause the herd to spook and start a stampede that would run the pounds off of his cows. He was watching Jones closely and, if he hadn't been desperate for hands, would have fired him the first week they were out of Texas. But Plott needed every man he could get who was willing to spend time in a saddle pushing his herd toward Kansas, and as long as the brute didn't do too much damage to his other hands, Zachariah would continue to tolerate the young tough's rude behavior.

If, however, one of the other hands decided that he had put up with enough from Cork and decided to plug him, and he could do it without stampeding the herd, Plott would not only let him keep his job but would see to it that whoever did it would get a nice bonus in his pay-envelope at the end of the trail.

The rest of the crew were tolerable enough as far as Cole was concerned. He could never fully relax though with the knowlege that Adams's hired killers were on his trail and Jones was trying to work up the nerve to brace him.

It was on a Tuesday night that everything came together and forced him into a gunfight. After putting in another hard day in the saddle Cole was about to slide into his bedroll for a few hours of sleep when he spotted a rattlesnake with a missing rattle coiled inside his blanket. Some folks would have claimed that Jackson was uncommon lucky to have found it before it struck him—others would have said he was gifted with a "second sight." The more religous would have said that he had a guardian angel looking after him. Cole would have pointed out that he had felt his blanket move when he touched it.

Finding snakes someone had stuck in his bedroll was nothing new to cowboys on the trail—it was a common practice among those prone to playing jokes among their fellow riders. But it was customary for safety's sake to use a rat snake or some other non-poisonous type of serpent to play the joke. Using a poisonous snake was not only dangerous for the man the joke was being played on, but the man foolish enough to handle the snake while playing the joke. Cole had been willing to think that Cork was just plain stupid, but when he saw that the "button" had been cut off the snake's tail he knew that Jones had intended that he get bitten by the rattler.

Noticing the commotion, Plott ran over to finish off the slithering serpent before one his men got spooked and started blasting away at it with his pistol and accidentally ended up shooting one of the other riders and spooking the herd. Everyone breathed a sigh of relief when Zachariah smashed the snake's head with a rock; they knew the havoc that a maddened rattler could cause as it crawled through camp in the dark—especially one with its rattle cut off so no one could hear it. The only one who appeared to be enjoying the whole episode was Cork Jones, who was laughing the whole time.

"What's the matter, Jackson? I would have thought that the brother of the famous Ethan Jackson could have scared that snake to death just by looking at it."

It was obvious from Cork's reaction that he had been the one who had put the snake in Cole's bedroll. Plott looked at the young cowhand in disgust. It no longer mattered that he was short-handed, he was going to fire the loudmouthed fool now. He had just opened his mouth to do so when Cole spoke up. "Jones you been on the prod for trouble ever since I joined the outfit, and since I don't want to find no more rattlers in my blanket and I don't figure that you're going to get any smarter or change your ways no time soon, I reckon that in the morning you and me will ride a mile back from the herd and I'll give you that gunfight you're dying to get."

The sneering Cork rapidly changed the expression on his face as he heard Jackson's words and looked into a pair of eyes that were staring holes through him.

Plott interrupted Cole by saying, "Make that two miles, Jackson," and then turning to Jones, he said, "Cork, make sure that you take your gear with you when you ride out in the morning. If you win, keep on riding—you're fired!" Then, addressing both Jackson and Jones, he said, "Make durn sure that neither one of you boys botch the job tomorrow and end up wounding each other; I don't have the time or inclination to nursemaid some shot-up cowboy all the way to Kansas." In a rare moment of generosity, he added, "Don't worry about the coyotes and such a chewin' on your dead bodies. I will stop long enough to put the loser—or losers—under the ground before we move on to Dodge City."

Cole was fortunate that he didn't have all of the dead men that his older brother had to haunt his dreams at night, so he dropped right off to sleep without giving the gunfight he was scheduled for in the morning a second thought. But as soon as he rose the next morning he remembered what had happened the night before and checked his Schofield to make sure that it was in top shape. Satisfied, Cole strapped on the weapon and walked over to the campfire where Plott was waiting for him.

"Looks like you're not too worried about facing Cork this morning," said the trail boss.

"My pa would have told you that was because I was just too stupid to know any better. But, yeah, I'm concerned about facing any man who's determined to kill me. I'd have to be a complete idiot not to be worried, but I don't see no way to avoid the fight."

Smiling, Plott said, "Oh, there's a way out of it all right and Jones thought of it last night."

"What do you mean?" asked Cole.

"Cork packed up his gear and rode off last night. The boy was a lot smarter than I gave him credit for. Of course, after I'd paid him the wages he had comin' last night he really didn't have no reason to hang around and I told him so."

Everything settled down after that. Cole noted that it was downright amazing how things smoothed out once the source of trouble was removed from a situation—whether it was man, beast, or lack of rain during a drought.

The rest of the drive to Dodge City was physically hard and draining on the spirit and mind with the occasional brush with death thrown in just to spice things up along the trail. After two months of that kind of life, the cowboys were ready to cut loose and celebrate, and Dodge was a town designed to let them do just that—within reason. It was also designed to keep order among the wild trail hands and separate them from their hard-earned cash.

Jackson was more than happy to see the end of the trail, even though it meant that he would have to start thinking about what he was going to do next. Up to that point all he had to do was stay on his horse as it pushed a bunch of cows in a northerly direction. By the very fact of having reached where he had been heading, he was being forced to think and plan once again, and Cole had never considered thinking to be his strong suit.

That wasn't the only thing that had been worrying him lately, for he had been hearing things about Ethan that he was finding hard to believe. He'd heard around Dodge that his brother had settled in a mining town where he was prospecting for gold while a schoolteacher had taken on the job as sheriff. And while it was said that Ethan still wore a gun, he had pretty much given up using it. That sure didn't sound like the brother Cole remembered.

Zachariah Plott had sold half of his herd to an eastern buyer when he got a telegram from an old friend offering him five dollars more a head for his remaining beeves if he could stay in Dodge City for another week until his friend could arrive with the money.

His friend had also offered to hire on some of Plott's hands if they wanted a few more weeks' work driving the cattle to the new owner's ranch. Having failed to get the hoped-for twenty dollars a head for his cattle, Plott was more than eager to accommodate his old friend's wishes and stay in town for an extra week. Knowing which of his men were prone to gamble or otherwise squander the money they'd been paid that would be needed to support them and and their families through the rest of the year in Texas, he'd sent those men back to his ranch in Texas and kept only a skeleton crew of his most stable hands. Jackson was the youngest of Plott's crew picked to stay in Kansas.

Happy to have his decision making postponed for a bit longer, Cole was relaxing in one of Dodge's many saloons when a familiar face appeared above the bat-wing doors of the saloon and Cork Jones pushed his ample bulk through the opening. He was followed by a hatchet-faced man wearing a tied-down gun. Jones's companion was whipcord thin and had a pale face that testified to the fact that whatever he did for a living it didn't involve him spending much time in the sun. His features were so chiseled that his face reminded Jackson of the blade of a single-bitted axe, but it was his eyes that Jackson took notice of. It was almost as if they were afire—not with life, but with pure hatred. Cole also noticed that his hand always hung close to the grip of the tied-down Colt on his leg, the fingers of his gunhand constantly flexing as he scanned the room until his eyes rested on Cole Jackson.

The gunman's name was Billy Hanks, a man well known for his love of killing. Over the years he had been so skilled at his job that he had come to be known as something of a sure-thing killer; in other words, if you definitely wanted someone dead, you hired Hanks and he made sure that you got what you wanted.

The only time Billy Hanks had been known to fail on a job occurred during a range war in Kansas where he'd been put on the payroll of a big rancher. He had been assigned to kill all those who opposed the rancher growing even bigger. The man at the top of that particular list was Ethan Jackson, who'd taken on the job of sheriff. And it would be Jackson who taught Hanks that there were men who were faster with a gun than he was. While Billy would have liked to have believed that Jackson putting a slug a couple of inches from his heart was only his bad luck, he knew deep in his heart that Ethan was and would probably always be better with a Colt than he was.

Billy had come away from the showdown learning a very valuable lesson: if you want to live a long life as a gunslinger—don't take unnecessary chances like taking on a skilled gunfighter in a straight-up fight. If a man planned to make his living handling a gun, he needed to learn to take every advantage he could. It was a lesson that stood Billy in good stead for many years thereafter.

Every time Billy now thought about rushing a job, his mind would flash back to that late afternoon in Kansas he had picked a fight with Jackson. The first hint he had that Jackson was not an ordinary gunslinger was his calm demeanor. Most men got nervous when they faced a professional gunman and had to be pushed a bit to get them to fight; especially when that fight might very well end up getting them killed. But Ethan Jackson was a different kind of man. Not that he'd ever enjoyed killing another man, but he'd had enough encounters with the lawless to know when to stop trying to talk to them and start throwing lead in their direction.

Billy had approached the table where Ethan was sitting

with his back to the wall so he could watch who came into the saloon. It was Hanks's intention to taunt Ethan and force him into a fight, but before he even opened his mouth, Ethan said, "Save your breath, Hanks. I know you've been paid to try and kill me. Well, you came looking for a fight—and you've found it."

Taken aback by Jackson's nonchalant attitude, Billy took a couple of seconds before he spoke. "That's right, Jackson, I'm calling you out."

"The street?" asked Jackson.

Nodding, the professional killer turned and walked out of the saloon into the street. Then he turned and headed toward the setting sun so he knew the bright light would be in his opponent's eyes.

Finishing his beer, Ethan followed behind him with his wide-brimmed Stetson pulled down low over his eyes to shade them from the sun.

With his feet spread apart, Hanks settled into his fighting stance and watched as Ethan walked out into the middle of the street with no more concern showing on his face than a farmer getting ready to slop the hogs. He certainly didn't look like a man getting ready to engage in a life-or-death struggle. But it was the way in which he spoke his next few words that really unnerved Billy: "Anytime you're ready, gunslinger."

Ethan was completely confident in his ability with a six-gun, and it came across in his voice. So much so that the tiny hairs on the back of Hanks's neck stood at attention, and his sixth sense screamed at him to make a run for it. But his pride and his faith in his own ability kept him rooted to the spot he'd picked to make his stand. Jackson remained calm as if he didn't have a care in the world.

Usually it was the other man who would nervously telegraph the fact that he was about to draw in some manner like the twitch of a finger or a raised eyebrow, but Jackson was giving nothing away. With Billy not able to see his eyes because of Ethan's pulled-down hat brim, it was Hanks who was growing nervous.

For the first time Hanks felt the throat-gripping fear he'd caused in so many other men—and he didn't like it one bit. Wanting the feeling to end, he made a grab for his pistol, hoping he wasn't telegraphing his draw by some movement of his body.

While Hanks was very fast, he wasn't a match for Jackson. He felt the slug slam into his chest at the same time he saw the orange flame blossom from Ethan's gun barrel.

Hanks was carried off to the doctor's office, where he would spend the next week wavering between life and death, while Jackson hung around town long enough to bring peace to the community. Then Jackson went on his way, ready to hire out his gun to the next town needing a peace officer.

Billy had carried a grudge against Jackson ever since that day. He tried hard but could not figure a way to get even, since Ethan was so much faster with a gun than he was and too alert to be taken from ambush.

Such were his thoughts when he saw Cole's face, which, while not being all that much like his brother's, was close enough for Hanks to notice a family resemblance on close inspection. He was pleased to think that he was about to finally get the revenge he craved, but was even happier to think about all the money he was about to make. With any luck at all, his temporary partner, Cork Jones, would end up taking the fall—if charges were brought—for what he was about to be very well paid to do.

Hanks had met Cork Jones several weeks earlier when he'd arrived in Dodge ahead of the cattle drive. It wasn't long, with the aid of a lot of whiskey, before Jones had told the entire story of his dispute with Jackson. Being drunk, he hadn't even bothered to try and lie about any part of the story to make himself look better.

Usually after getting the information about the location of a target, Hanks would have dumped the friendship act, but the story Cork had told him gave the killer an idea about how to do his job without bringing unwanted attention to himself—always a good idea when in a town with as much law as Dodge City.

Hanks had begun thinking of the $1,000 bounty that Andy Adams had put on Jackson's head as belonging to him already. All he had to do was get Cork Jones to gun Cole down, dig up the body and cut off his head, throw it into some chemicals he'd bought from a doctor to preserve it, and carry it back to Adams in Ohio.

With that goal in mind, Hanks had been teaching a very slow and clumsy Jones how to use a gun well enough to take on Jackson in a gunfight. It was a simple enough plan, but Hanks didn't have all that much faith in his pupil's ability with a short-gun; if he hadn't been so concerned about what the law might of had to say, he would have taken on Jackson by himself.

There was also the problem of Cole's older brother. Billy had heard the rumors of Ethan taking up the peaceful life, but he had no desire to have him on his trail looking to avenge his younger brother's death. Unless he absolutely had to, Hanks planned to restrict his part in the enterprise to teaching Jones how to use a gun.

Hanks was a very greedy man, however, and his lust for money had overruled his common sense on more than one occasion. It did again this night as he followed Cork into the saloon. He knew that the smart thing for him to do was give Jones his chance at Jackson, and then, if necessary, ambush Jackson sometime later. But he was in a hurry and wanted to end it now.

Because a professional gunman had been working with him for a few weeks, Cork thought that he now had the edge on Cole. He was smiling and confident as he walked up to Jackson's table and said, "Thought you could get away from me by running off the way you did, didn't you?"

Smelling the whiskey on Jones, Cole figured that Cork had found his courage in a bottle. He wondered if this speech was meant to impress the crowd, or if he had drunk so much rotgut that he'd actually begun to believe that it *hadn't* been him who had sneaked off in the middle of the night. If he was able to convince himself of that, he wouldn't have any trouble convincing himself that he was a gunfighter.

Cole could tell that there was no point in trying to talk Jones out of the fight—and if the truth had been told, he wasn't all that inclined to do so anyway. Pushing back his chair, Jackson got to his feet and stood toe-to-toe with the red-faced Jones. "All right, Cork," he said. "Let's get to it."

As he looked into the hard eyes of Cole Jackson, Cork once again began to panic, and his mind began to race in an attempt to find a way out of the hole he had dug for himself. Then, remembering that he wasn't alone this time, he glanced over at Hanks, who nodded. Jones took notice that his twitching gunhand was no longer twitching but was gripping the rosewood handle of his Colt.

Smiling nervously, Cork said, "All right, Jackson, any time you're ready."

Chapter Ten
The Expedition

Ethan said goodbye to Corey O'Brien, turned his horse in the direction of Fort Laramie, and "sank spur." They had been five miles outside of Leantown when they parted; Corey would take his time riding back to his home while Jackson would be riding for the fort as fast as his horse could carry him. The reason for the deception was to allow Ethan to return to the place in the Big Horn Mountains where he had found gold without being trailed by a herd of unwanted gold seekers.

He had already picked out the men who he wanted to accompany him on the expedition and sent them out two days ahead of him with packhorses and mining supplies. He had instructed them to ride in a westerly direction to fool anybody who might be following them and then to turn east for Fort Laramie where they would all join up and head for the mountains. The members of the expedition who were taking the long way to the fort were Caleb Kenton, his seventeen-year-old son named Ezekial, and Jake Collins. John Baldwin had been invited to accompany them but he felt that the town wouldn't be safe if he were to leave for very long.

Ethan had considered taking more men into the mountains with him, but word had been circulating that the tribes, because the Army was chasing them after Custer's massacre, were on the run, with many of them heading for Canada. With the tribes scattering in different directions, Jackson figured that there was little chance of a band of braves wanting to take on three men with lever-action Winchesters. Kenton had retired his squirrel rifle for new repeaters for himself and Ezekial, but Collins still clung to his trusty .45–.70 Sharps.

While Ethan's expedition was small in number, it was well equipped when it came to firearms, and with men who had the skill and guts to use them. Jackson figured that any war party large enough to try and take them on had better figure on ending up as a smaller war party when the smoke cleared.

The plan was simple. They would all join up at the fort where Ethan would guide them to the spot where he had made his find the previous year. If the rest of the ore beneath the boulders was as rich as the dirt he'd found under the first one, Jackson figured that a month of intensive mining might produce as much as forty thousand dollars in raw gold. If he could find where the gold originated, he figured on possibly doubling that amount.

The first thing he planned to do was to mail two letters he had written. He'd had plenty of time during the winter to think and come up with plans to improve and help the settlement to prosper, but every idea he had thought of required the same thing—money. Everything depended on whether or not he could make his discovery in the Big Horns pay off.

The first letter he had written was addressed to his father back in Ohio. The opening part of the letter had been written during the middle of winter and was filled with news about what Ethan had been up to since he'd last sent a letter back east. By necessity it was a thick letter since it had been some time since he had written. The second part of the letter had been written recently and recounted the stories he had been hearing about his brother Cole. Ethan wanted to know what had happened back in Ohio.

The second letter was addressed to an old friend known as Taw Skerns, a good man Ethan hadn't seen for over five years when he had pulled up stakes and headed for Alaska. Jackson had come up with an idea that he was sure would appeal to someone of Skern's adventurous and entrepreneurial spirit, and had outlined his idea in detail in the letter. He had promised Taw nothing but a chance to do something in the Wyoming territory that no one else had done before and the opportunity to risk his life on an almost daily basis if he were so inclined.

With mail service at the time covering a good part of the country, Jackson felt that there was a good chance that he would recieve an answer to his letters within a month or less. By that time, Ethan figured that he would either be making plans to marry Sharon and fixing to make a life for them in Leantown, or he would be packing up and heading for some place where he could make a living. The only part of his plan that was definite was the fact that he was going to marry Sharon.

As to his reputation as a gunfighter, he figured that if he could keep from using his gun as he had been, there was a possibility that people might begin to lose interest in him and he and his new family might be able to settle down and live in peace—at least he hoped that that would be the case. With Baldwin patrolling the town and maintaining a law and order that wouldn't tolerate gunfights as ordinary every-day occurrences, there was a good chance that he might be able to remain peaceable and stay alive at the same time.

Two days later, Ethan rode into Fort Laramie and posted his two letters. He then went in search of the nearest establishment that sold whiskey and reunited with Jake Collins.

"Did you enjoy all the sights on your way from Leantown?" asked Jake as he downed the whiskey from the shot glass he was holding.

Smiling, Ethan said, "As much of it as I could take in while riding at a full gallop for most of the way."

"Well, you and your horse can rest up tonight and we can all head out for the Big Horns in the morning. Caleb and his boy are a rarin' to hit the trail."

"Good," Jackson said. He then ordered a beer and joined Jake at his table in an effort to wash down some trail dust.

At first light the next morning, four well-armed and well-provisioned gold hunters rode out of Fort Laramie in hopes of getting rich. Ethan and Caleb, as usual, were alert as they rode along, but Jake was recovering from a hangover, while young Ezekial was bleary-eyed from a night spent awake over the excitement about going on his first gold hunt. It was an experience that every other man on the expedition had already gone through at one time or another, and every one of them knew that Ezekial would have a very hard time rolling out of bed the next morning after he'd spent a sleepless night. They also knew what that first glimpse of gold would do to him when he found that first nugget in his pan. None of the men had any trouble remembering what their first time was like, for they experienced it all over again every time they set eyes on gold in a pan that they were swirling in front of them.

Each man also had his own private dreams about what he planned to do with the gold he found. Caleb planned to use his to buy a sawmill and expand his construction business. As soon as he could find some men who didn't have the gold fever, he planned to hire them and put them to work at his new business. Kenton's plan therefore wasn't to ride into the mountains and risk his life in an effort to get rich, but to get capital to invest in an enterprise that would not only put food on his table but would, with careful management, put food on his grandchildren's table for many years to come.

Jake was on the trip because it was something exciting to do and gold fever was an ailment he'd picked up during his youth. As far as he was concerned, that was enough of a reason to ride along. He also planned to invest whatever gold he found into Ethan's schemes of building up Leantown. From the way Ethan had described his ideas to him, it seemed like they might just work. At any rate, it would be a whole lot of fun to see how they turned out.

Ethan's plan was to start a large cattle ranch on some of the hundreds of acres he had seen in the sheltered valley. With Jake putting his share of the gold into such an operation, the herd would grow at a faster rate and start producing profits that could be plowed back into the enterprise and cause it to grow even more rapidly. There was plenty of open land around Leantown where more ranches could be started, both large and small, and the population in that part of the territory would grow by leaps and bounds.

Ethan had told his plan to exactly four people: Jake, Kenton, Baldwin, and Sharon O'Brien. All of them agreed that it was a good idea. Jake pointed out that it was not only a good idea, but that it was the type of idea that would either make him a very rich and powerful man in the territory or, depending on blizzards, droughts, and predators, would end up completely bankrupting the ambitious former lawman.

Jackson readily agreed that his idea of a cattle ranch in

such a wild and isolated part of the country was a real gamble where the weather and nature in general could be so unpredictable. But he figured on hedging his bets by locating his ranch within the confines of the protected valley where bone-chilling winds could be blocked. He planned to further protect his investment by contracting with Kenton, who, with his hardworking sons, was to build a barn and line shacks in which to both store grain and hay to help feed the cattle through the winter, and house cowboys to watch over the stock.

He'd also spoken with Caleb about designing some sheltered enclosures in which to house the cattle during blizzards that had previously wiped out other such enterprises. It was a completely new idea and a very different way of doing things on the frontier than the customary way of letting nature take its course and allowing only the strong to survive. In one way that sort of an attitude made sense; especially for those who were native to the west and had been brought up almost as hard as the wild animals running over the land. But to someone like Ethan who had been brought up on a farm back east the idea of investing in a crop, whether it was a potato patch or a herd of milk cows, and then allowing it to go untended or fend for itself was just plain stupid behavior.

Back home in Ohio barns were built not only to store hay but to house the animals during inclement weather. Even the lowly tomato plant had the weeds cut from around it and stakes driven beside it to support it during high winds and when the vines started to bear the heavy fruit. To his father the way that ranchers treated their animals in the west would have been similar to him throwing corn on untilled soil and letting it grow on its own—it would have been a waste of seed, ground, and effort.

So Jackson, while trying to think of some way to keep

Leantown alive, thought of putting some of the techniques he had learned on his father's farm to good use in Wyoming. The plan was a good one and had been well thought out. Everything now depended on whether or not they found enough gold.

This time, Ethan had made sure that they were well-outfitted with shovels, picks, and pans; not to mention a generous supply of lumber with which they could build a couple of sluice boxes to wash out the gold they shoveled from the creek. Those two boxes would permit them to be much faster and efficient in the gold recovery operation. And that was important, for while most of the hostiles had scattered with a vengeful cavalry pursuing them, that didn't mean that there couldn't be a war party or two running loose in the Big Horns eager to add to their victory over Custer at Little Big Horn.

Jackson's party was even taking the precaution of not using their rifles to shoot game. Kenton had a bow and some Cherokee-made arrows that he planned to use to take some rabbits and other small game with, thereby keeping the group in fresh meat without giving their position away to whoever else might be in the mountains. Ethan had seen Caleb use the bow before and he figured that between Kenton's skill with arrows and a creek that would be full of trout, there was little chance that they would ever go hungry during their stay.

The country they were travelling through was beautiful—so beautiful that Jackson pushed his thoughts of commerce aside to concentrate on the beautiful scenery he was riding past. His relaxed mood didn't last for very long, however, for while looking toward a distant hill, he spotted a lone Indian looking back at him. He didn't need the field glasses in his saddlebags this time to make out who it was observing their progress up the branch—he had seen him several times around Leantown during the winter. It was the same brave he had left tied to a tree in the mountains a year ago.

Riding up beside Ethan, Jake asked, "Friend of yours?"

Scratching his head, Ethan answered, "Can't say exactly what he is. The last time we met he tried to stick me with his skinning knife and ended up getting knocked out and tied to a tree while I made my way back to the fort on foot. For some reason he's been dogging my trail ever since."

"Well, I can tell you a couple of things about your friend up there: the first is that he ain't afraid of us a seein' him, and second, if'n he plans on takin' revenge for what you did, he's one patient and determined red man."

Nothing happened during the rest of the day, and by that evening they had reached the spot Jackson had named "Boulder Branch." Taking his companions to the place where he had dug up the $500 worth of gold, Ethan told them about how rich the spot had been in ore. When the three men had seen the circular area of three foot diameter and were told about how much gold had been dug from that hole, they literally flew to the task of assembling two sluice boxes from the lumber that they had packed in, cutting long and thick saplings to use as pry bars in the morning as soon as there was light enough in the sky for them to start working.

Jackson had to almost physically restrain Ezekial from turning over one of the boulders that evening, knowing that the next thing that he would want to do would be to start panning out some of the creek gravel by lantern light. It wasn't that Ethan wanted to dampen the young man's enthusiasm for work, but he didn't favor lighting up the night in hostile territory; especially since he knew that at least one hostile was watching them already. Jackson had no intention of providing him with a lit-up target to shoot at from the cover of darkness.

To help calm the younger Kenton, Ethan took him upstream to introduce him to the pleasures of fishing for mountain trout with a hook baited with jerky. Ezekial was still pretty excited just to be there, but after pulling a couple of large trout from the stream he started to settle down a bit and concentrate on the job at hand of feeding four hungry men, their appetites whetted from hard traveling and the fresh mountain air.

Caleb took a trip downstream with his bow and came back with a rabbit to add to the pot. Jackson understood his companions' eagerness and, as far as he was concerned, he wished that enough daylight had been left for him to have ridden upstream to look for the spot where the gold originated. But tomorrow morning they would begin working as two-man teams, digging under the boulders and washing the ore out in the sluice boxes where they were reasonably sure that gold was located. They would have been foolish to have gone looking for gold somewhere that wasn't a sure bet and leave behind an area where there was almost a guarantee they would find some of the yellow metal. Still, Jackson felt an overpowering urge to explore upstream, and if he had been alone—he would have.

Ezekial had been given the first watch that night because of him being so keyed up. Everybody knew that he would have to calm down before he could ever drop off to sleep. By the time his father's turn to stand guard had rolled around, the younger Kenton was more than ready to crawl into his bedroll.

The night passed without incident, and Jackson was told so by Collins as he waked him to stand the final watch a few hours before daybreak. Jackson had picked the last watch for himself since that seemed like the time most things happened, whether it was the time that men liked to schedule hangings or Indians preferred to attack.

No attack came, and those who were still sleeping were awakened by the smell of coffee boiling and bacon frying. Ethan knew that he wouldn't have to wake up Jake and Caleb; he knew that the smell of the coffee and bacon would do that for him. Even the tantalizing smells of a breakfast cooked by somebody else weren't enough to stir a sleep-starved teenage boy from his night's slumber though, as Ezekial continued to make up for his previous lack of sleep.

Noticing that his son was still in his bedroll, Caleb walked up to him and prodded him with the toe of his boot. "Get up, son, it's time to go to work."

But Ezekial only rolled over and mumbled, "Be right there, Pa," and then promptly started to doze off again.

Winking at Ethan, Collins said, "Let the poor boy sleep, Caleb. He's just not as interested in looking for that gold as the rest of us are."

Ezekial was almost asleep, but as soon as he heard the word gold he came wide awake, threw his blanket aside and jumped to his feet ready to start digging. Not that he looked all that able with his face puffed out the way it was from sleeping. His face was so badly swollen, in fact, that he looked like he had slept with a hornet's nest for a pillow.

The boy started out slowly, but once he drank half a cup of Jackson's cowboy coffee they almost had to sit on him to make him take the time to eat some breakfast. Ethan knew that it was real important to get some food down the youngster's throat that morning, for once they started to find gold none of them would be wanting to stop for lunch, and by the end of the day, when darkness would force them to stop working, they would be too tired to eat anything. Ethan knew that a lack of sleep, food, and enough rest could tear down a man's health faster than most diseases, and a sick man in the mountains where every gun might be needed was a serious threat to their survival.

Finally, with everybody's stomach reasonably full, the men began their first day of operation. Caleb and his son chose the nearest boulder to turn over while Jackson and Jake picked a large stone a few feet upstream. Ezekial, with young and eager eyes, was the first of the group to spot a gold nugget glittering under the water. To satisfy all of their curiosities and to accommodate the boy's youthful enthusiasm, it was decided that they would clean up the sluice boxes after only two hours of shoveling dirt through them to see how well they were doing. Usually a cleanup wasn't done until the end of a day's work; sometimes a cleanup was put off until the end of the week. But that always gave a thief more of a chance to sneak off with some rich dirt to pan, and it was a practice that only the most lazy, or stupid, miners chose to engage in. Jackson always favored doing a cleanup at the end of the day.

Caleb, with his son spurring him on, was the first to get a pan of the concentrate to swirl in the creek. Working the pan in a back-and-forth motion, it wasn't long before he had reduced the contents of the pan to a black sand liberally speckled with match-head-sized flakes and nuggets with gold dust riding the bottom edge.

Seeing the gold, Ezekial let out a loud whoop that could have been heard for a mile or more. "Ezekial!" growled Caleb in a low angry voice. "You don't have to tell the whole country about what we just found!"

Ezekial's face colored a dark red as he apologized. "Sorry, Pa. I just wasn't thinking."

Laughing, Jake said, "That's okay, son. I've seen many a grown man get so excited the first time he saw half as much gold as you've got in that there pan that he let out a whoop, drew his pistol, and started throwing lead every which a way. I remember one fool who got so durn excited that he actually shot off his own durn toe."

Ethan, after giving his pan one final swirl, walked over to where his friends were gathered to take a look and show them what he had panned out. Jackson had not only found a similar amount and type of gold as that recovered by the Kentons, but he had also found a nugget the size of a man's thumb. Eyes got wide and there was an audible gasp from Ezekial as they all gathered around Ethan to gawk at the nugget. They passed it among themselves in almost religious reverence.

Nothing more was said as they returned to their work and began digging at a feverish pace; one of them digging under the boulder they had overturned, emptying one shovelfull of dirt after another into the sluice box, then pouring water over it, while his partner rocked the box back and forth to wash the lighter dirt back into the stream.

Both teams worked at a fevered pitch, with the older Collins matching the younger and more agile Ezekial shovel for shovel and rocking the sluice box with as much enthusiasm as a man half his age. As Jackson had expected, none of them wanted to stop working long enough to eat lunch that afternoon, so they kept working until darkness called an end to the day's mining.

It took three weeks of hard labor until the gold fever abated enough to let them think about anything besides digging and washing out gold. And it was then that they realized how tired they were of eating nothing but beans and jerky and how much they would really like to sit down to a meal of fresh meat.

Ethan never ceased to be amazed about how hard a man would work when gold was at stake. He was unable to think of anybody who would work as hard as a prospector when there was a whiff of gold in the air. Even a man who might be known as the laziest man in the territory would work himself into a frenzy to dig gold out of the ground. A man who was a hard worker to begin with could, and had, worked himself to death in the goldfields.

It was hard for Caleb Kenton to put down his shovel and take up his bow to go in search of game to give everybody a much-needed change in diet. As hard as it was for him, it was almost impossible to get his young son to leave the creek and set out snares to trap game. This resulted in Ezekial not being as alert as he should have been as he set snares and deadfalls along the game trails he was walking.

Jackson was finding it hard to stop thinking about gold himself, and while he had ridden upstream with the intention of setting a few traps, he was alert for any place where there might be a likely spot to find more gold.

As for Jake, there was something else that had aroused his curiosity and it had been irritating him to the point where he had begun to think of it as an itch that was just going to have to be scratched.

Toward evening all of them had started to drift back toward camp—except for Ezekial, who after setting his traps had leaned up against a tree to rest. Without the stimulation of digging for gold to keep him awake, he had drifted off to sleep.

Back at camp Collins was the next to last to return. He didn't pack any game with him like the three rabbits Kenton had arrowed and was now skinning by the cook fire, but he did have the solution to a mystery that had been puzzling Ethan for over a year.

"Ran into your shadow farther up on the mountain today, Ethan," he said, reaching for the coffeepot at the edge of the fire.

Knowing that Jake was referring to the warrior who had

been following him, Jackson asked, "What did my friend have to say; he want another crack at me?"

Sipping the hot coffee, Jake said, "Not hardly. It seems that you've confused him by what you did back here in the mountains last year when you killed his two companions and tied him to that tree instead of killing him. That's not something that an Indian would have done, so he figures that you must either be crazy or protected by some sort of powerful medicine that would let you act the way you do."

"But why's he been doggin' my trail?"

Laughing, Jake said, "Funny that you put it that way, since that brave goes by the name of 'Limping Dog' because of a bad leg and his habit of never giving up on something—sort of like a hound chasing a rabbit." Taking a drink of the strong coffee, Jake continued. "It's not all that unusual for an Injun to get notional about something and follow along behind somebody or something until they figure it out—sometimes to their dying day."

"How'd you explain what I did to him?"

"Couldn't. I tried to explain to him about how the white man believed in fair play and all but he just said that a people who believed in such a thing must have madness in them and the purpose of fighting was to kill an enemy, and how that anyone who believed otherwise had to be 'tetched.' "

"He plannin' on makin' any trouble for us?" asked Kenton, who was beginning to get concerned that his son hadn't shown up yet.

"Nope. At least not as long as Ethan is with us. He figures that the Great Spirit must be lookin' after somebody as crazy as our good friend Ethan here, and he doesn't want to anger his god by attacking somebody who has that kind of protection, or his friends either. As a matter of fact, he took the trouble to warn me that there was a large party of

Cheyenne that would be passing through here in a couple of days and he suggested that it would be a real good idea if we weren't here when they showed up—I tend to agree with that opinion."

Watching Kenton who had walked to the edge of camp and was staring off into the distance, Ethan asked, "How much of that gold you figure we've taken out so far?"

Collins didn't have to think very long to answer the question, since he had been weighing the amount that was mined at the end of each day and had filed away the numbers in a memory that was as accurate and up to date as any cattleman's tally book. "About twenty-four thousand, the best I can figure," he answered.

"Real close to what I was counting on and it's real hard for a dead man to spend his money—no matter how much of it he has. I reckon the best thing to do is pack up tonight and ride out of here in the morning; everybody agree with that?"

"Yep," said Jake.

"Reckon so," added Caleb.

Looking around, for the first time Ethan noticed that the younger Kenton hadn't returned to camp yet. "Where's your boy, Caleb?" he asked.

"We separated. I went hunting and he took off to set some traps and snares. But he should have been back here long before now."

Ezekial was getting worried about being late getting back to camp, and the fact that none of the snares he'd set had caught any game didn't make him feel any better about the situation. After all, what kind of a man goes out with the intention of catching game for the pot and ends up falling asleep on the trail—what would Jake and Mr. Jackson have to say about that? Worse, what would his pa have to say?

With his shoulders slumped and his head down, Ezekial stood on the cliff above camp and looked down at the men who he would be trying to explain his actions to. Ideas suddenly began forming in his mind—ideas about how best to present his case. Those thoughts were interrupted by a loud woof that came from behind him, and then there was the sound of something popping. Turning slowly around, Kenton found himself not more than fifteen feet from a boar grizzly which, when it stood on its hind legs, appeared to be at least eight feet tall.

While Ezekial had been smart enough to bring his gun along with him, he knew that the bear would be on him before he could even jack a shell into the rifle's chamber. Turning back around he noticed the tops of the pine trees growing beside the cliff. Ordinarily, the idea of jumping from the top of a cliff in the hope of the branches of the trees below him breaking his fall would have seemed foolish, but with a snarling bruin about to make a meal out of him, the treetops below were beginning to look downright inviting.

He heard the roar, felt the hot breath on his back, and smelled the bear's fetid stench—it was more than enough to help him make up his mind. Flinging the rifle out in front of him, he leapt for the nearest treetop and yelled out, "Pa!"

Ezekial didn't have to yell to bring attention to himself, for the three men's attention had been riveted to the top of the cliff as soon as they heard the bear roar.

Dropping back to all fours, the grizzly moved over to the edge of the cliff to watch as Ezekial crashed through the branches of the pine until he hit the ground, stunned and unable to move.

Moving its dish-shaped head back and forth, the bear let

out another earthshaking roar and charged down the side of the cliff in pursuit of its stubborn prey.

Moving the fastest that either Jake or Ethan had ever seen a human move in their lives, Caleb rushed to where his son had come to rest at the base of the pine. The grizzly arrived at the foot of the cliff at the same time. Jacking a shell into his Winchester, Caleb fired and kept firing until the weapon was empty.

Kenton had emptied the Winchester, but instead of killing the beast, he'd only succeded in drawing its attention toward him. It began to lumber in his direction, determined to rip apart its tormenter.

Drawing his knife, Caleb got ready to fight the maddened bear hand-to-claw. They were no more than five feet apart when Kenton began to see little puffs of dirt start to explode on the grizzly's shoulder. He then began to hear the shots coming from his right. Turning in that direction, he could see that Ethan was working the lever of his Winchester as fast as he could.

Jackson had also emptied his rifle and, as Kenton had done, only succeeded in turning the beast's rage on another target—himself. The only weapon left to Ethan was his revolver, and while such a weapon was not preferred when facing a maddened grizzly, Jackson's instincts took over and he made the fastest draw that he had made in life. The bear wasn't impressed by his skill—or affected by the five 255-grain slugs that had entered the armor-like hide over its heart. He continued to plod forward with fire blazing from pig-like eyes and the intention of tearing Jackson limb from limb.

Out of the corner of his eye Ethan could see Caleb rushing toward the bear with his knife held in front of him. He knew, however, that he would be dead before Caleb ever reached the bear—and so would Caleb if he tried taking on the thousand-pound behemoth with nothing more than a knife. Locking eyes with the charging beast, Ethan resigned himself to dying—but then the bear suddenly went still and slowly fell right at his feet.

Glancing down at the bear's prone body, he noticed that a good part of the animal's skull had been blown apart, and what was left was a large and bloody hole where its brain had once been.

"Dang close, weren't it?" said Jake as he walked up beside Ethan carrying his smoking .45–.70 Sharps.

"I reckon so," said Jackson.

"You reckon! Why son, if'n a man could carve a beefsteak that thin off'n a beeve he'd never have to kill the cow!"

Walking over to where Caleb was making sure that his son hadn't broken any bones or punctured any of his vital organs when he took his dive off the cliff, Jake spoke to the youngster. "Ezekial, the rest of us have been talking about whether or not we might ought to pull up stakes and head out of here before things get dangerous. How you feel about it?"

Still shaken from his fall, Ezekial managed to say, "Sounds like a real good idea to me."

Chapter Eleven
The Reunion

When the gold hunters rode out of the mountains the next morning, their pack animals were earning their keep and would appreciate their feed at the end of the trail, for they were packing a heavy load. Jake had been dead-on about how much the gold would be worth when it was weighed on offical scales. The final tally came to $24,000. That meant that every man who'd ridden up the creek leading to Boulder Branch three weeks earlier had earned around $6,000 each for less than a month's work. The work had been hard, but none of them complained about the working conditions. They'd gone so far as to agree that grizzly bears were an acceptable risk for the chance to make that kind of money.

They'd even been able to make use of the bear by skinning it out and giving the hide to Ezekial. All of them agreed that he had had the hardest and most dangerous part when it came to bringing the beast to ground—he'd been the bait.

While the load they were packing was heavy, they were still able to make it to Fort Laramie within three days. Once there, they converted the gold to cash and wired it to bankers in different parts of the country where each man was accustomed to doing business. It didn't take long for them to start spending their fortunes. Caleb Kenton immediately invested in a sawmill and had it shipped to Leantown, where he planned to start building the barn and shelters that he and Ethan had discussed. It would be a good start toward the business empire that he had been dreaming of putting together.

Ethan and Jake had decided to go in as partners on the cattle and felt that the best and fastest way to go about building a herd was to ride east to one of the cattle towns. There, buyers were showing up to buy the longhorns being driven up from Texas and also breeding stock. They knew that they would be paying a much higher price for the cows by doing it that way, but to go to Texas and buy cattle would throw their plans a year behind and they needed to get the operation up and running as soon as possible. There was also the consideration of the expenses involved when it came to hiring hands to drive the cattle and the possibility of losing the herd on the way up from Texas. Jackson and Collins had talked it over and decided that no man's luck could hold out forever, and with the kind of lives they had lived, their luck had been stretched about as far as it could go. The smartest thing for them to do, then, was pay the higher price and take less risk.

Both Collins and Jackson knew men in the cattle business, but Jake remembered that a good friend of his had talked about driving a herd up from his ranch that particular year, and Collins decided to send some telegrams to find out if he had done so. When he received word that that was indeed the case, a couple of more telegrams were exchanged between the old friends which resulted in Ethan and Jake agreeing to pay twenty dollars a head for five hundred head of mostly cows and some steers, provided that the owner would hold the herd in Dodge until they could get there. They also agreed to pay extra for some of the trail driver's hands to drive the cattle on up to Leantown.

That was the reason that Ethan was now standing in the saloon watching the little drama unfold in front of him. Two kids were about to draw down on each other. One of those kids was a brute who lacked not only the skill to be a gunfighter, but the guts as well. He'd seen the type many times before. He was the kind who, when sober, acted like the coward he truly was, but when fortified with whiskey or in the majority where he could draw strength from the crowd, he was eager to fight. Since he didn't have a crowd behind him or appear to be drunk, Ethan figured that there must be something else that was giving him the courage to brace somebody the way he was at the time.

Jackson's suspicions were confirmed when he saw the kid falter, look around the room for someone, and then, when he seemed satisfied, turn back to face the other kid with confidence. Taking a closer look at the crowd, Ethan found the reason the shaky gunman had got his nerve back: a sharp-faced man gripping the handle of his Colt. He recognized the man as Billy Hanks. It was an obvious setup—somebody really wanted that other kid dead. While Jackson knew that it was none of his business and that getting into a gunfight with somebody as famous as Billy Hanks would only add to the reputation that he was trying so hard to shed, he'd been a lawman for too long to just stand by and let a cold-blooded murder take place in front of him.

"Hello, Billy," Jackson said. His voice had been low, almost a whisper, but Hanks had heard it and he understood the threat that it carried. Jerking around, he stood facing a smiling Ethan whose thumbs were hooked in the front of his belt. Hanks began to sweat.

Ethan could see the fear in Hanks's eyes as he let go of the pistol's handle like he'd picked up the wrong end of a branding iron. Jackson could almost hear the wheels turning in the gunman's head as he figured the odds, and when he'd made the final tally about what his chances were when it came to drawing against Ethan, he tipped his hat to the ex-lawman and walked out the swinging doors of the saloon without so much as a glance in Cork Jones's direction.

Jones hadn't seen what had taken place between Hanks and Ethan. All he saw was Billy walking out of the saloon, leaving him to face Cole Jackson alone. His gut instinct told him to run. But Cork was tired of running. He'd run from a bunch of old men back home in Texas and, just a few weeks ago, he'd sneaked out of camp to avoid a gunfight.

But those old men back in Texas had stayed in Texas— they weren't traveling all over the country spreading stories about one of their own. And as for the cow camp, no one had seen him sneak out in the middle of the night; he could always make up some sort of a story to explain why he did that. This time he'd called out a man in front of witnesses; if he didn't stand up now, the only reputation he was going to get was for being the fastest man in the west when it came to backing down from a fight—a fight that he had started.

While Jones had begun to sweat buckets, Cole remained calm, his eyes narrowing, waiting for Cork to make his move. The calm that Cole was displaying further unnerved Jones to the point where he could no longer take the pressure. Letting out a desperate cry, he clawed for the gun at his side.

Ethan saw Cork make his desperate grab for the sidearm,

and while the other kid's draw was smooth and fluid, it was incredibly slow—too slow for a man who had gunslingers out to kill him. He made a note to tell the kid, if he survived the fight, that he would be better off finding somewhere to live where people didn't go around packing pistols.

Cole could see the desperation and fear in Jones's eyes, so even though he knew he was slow when it came to pulling the Schofield, he still took the time to aim carefully at Cork's arm so that he would only wound him.

A slug entered Jones's right shoulder, causing him to drop the pistol and sink into a nearby chair until some men helped him to the doctor's office up the street. A feeling of relief came over Cork so strong that he didn't even think about the pain the hole in his shoulder was causing him; at last he'd faced up to a man and survived a gunfight. He no longer had anything to prove to anybody. He could go on with his life.

And that was exactly what he did. He became known as a pillar of the community where he lived and fathered a passel of children who thought him the greatest man in the world. After digging the .44 slug from Cork's shoulder, the doctor had given it to him as a memento and Cork had developed the habit of carrying it around in his pocket. Every time he would feel the urge to throw his weight around, he would fondle that piece of lead to remind himself about how precious life was and how close he had come to losing it that day in the saloon.

After things had settled down, two men at the bar where Ethan was standing started talking. "I reckon his brother got all the speed in the family," said the man to Ethan's right.

"Looks like, but that Cole Jackson can sure shoot straight. Did you see where he put that bullet? Most folks would have emptied their pistols into that other kid's guts just as fast as they could have pulled the trigger."

Putting down the beer he was holding, Ethan asked, "Did you say Cole Jackson?"

"Yep," said the last man who spoke. "He's the brother of Ethan Jackson—you know, the famous gunfighter."

"Yeah, I've heard the name," said Ethan, who turned and started walking toward Cole's table.

Cole immediately tensed up as soon as he saw Ethan walking in his direction. He automatically figured that Ethan was another killer Andy Adams had put on his payroll. From the look of him, he appeared to be the type of man who could get the job done. Then, to Cole's astonishment, the killer's face broke out into a genuine smile.

"Hello, little brother," he said, extending his hand.

The way Cole's jaw dropped it appeared like he was trying to catch flies. "E . . . Ethan?" he stammered.

"That's right, Cole. I'm your older brother."

Numbly shaking Ethan's hand, he invited his brother to join him. Taking a seat, Ethan asked, "What are you doing in Dodge, little brother?"

Fortunately, Cole had now gotten over the shock of seeing his brother and had regained the power of speech, so he said, "I rode up here from Texas with a cattle outfit and we're waiting for a buyer to show up."

"Are you with Zachariah Plott's outfit?"

"How'd you know that?" asked Cole.

"Because I'm that buyer," Ethan answered. "One of them anyway."

"What are you doing buying cattle? The last I heard you were prospecting."

"I was. That's where I got the money to buy the cattle. Now I'm looking to start a ranch in Wyoming."

It took awhile for that idea to take root in Cole's brain.

He'd never known of his brother to have any ambitions about owning a ranch or any other kind of a business— he'd always made a living working as a sheriff or prospecting, and in his early days he'd worked as a trail hand. Now here he was, the famous Ethan Jackson, giving up sheriffing to live the settled life of a rancher. Cole couldn't have been more surprised if his father had told him that he was giving up farming, trading his plow for an apron, and starting a restaurant somewhere.

His thoughts were interrupted by Ethan asking a question. "I've been hearing about some mighty bad men doggin' your trail lately. What exactly happened back in Ohio anyway?"

After Cole recounted what had happened, Ethan said, "Well, little brother, you sure got yourself into some kind of a mess. And from what you just told me, I can't think of anywhere in the country where you'd be safe." Then, seeing the look of despair that came over Cole's face, he added, "Well, maybe one place."

"Where's that?"

Ethan's original thought had been a hermit's cave, but he was sure that his brother wouldn't appreciate his idea of humor just then, so he asked, "You got any plans, Cole?"

"Other than pushing Mr. Plott's . . . or should I say, your cattle on to Wyoming, I haven't planned on doing anything."

"How'd you like to come and work for me?"

"Doin' what?"

"Mostly cattle for right now, but I've got some ideas about building up the community where I live and I could use you to help me out with some of those ideas. I can promise you regular pay and, for the most part, regular meals. I'll even throw in a promise that you probably won't be bored."

Ethan could have added that he would also enjoy the benefits of his protection, but he didn't want Cole to think that he was treating him like he couldn't take care of himself. But with the kind of forces that were being brought against him, there was little chance that any man could survive without help. So he repeated his question. "What about it, Cole? You going on my payroll?"

Before Cole could answer, Jake Collins walked in with Zachariah Plott in tow. Crossing over to Ethan, Jake said, "Heard that there was some gunplay over here and that there was some hombre named Jackson who plugged a man. Looks like I can't seem to leave you for any time at all without you gettin' into some kind of a scrape, doesn't it."

"Wrong Jackson," said Ethan. Hooking his thumb in Cole's direction, he said, "Here's the gentleman who caused all the commotion. Jake, meet my brother, Cole." Introductions were made all around the table, and, after they all took seats, Jake said, "Well, now that all of the formalities are out of the way, let's get down to business."

"All right," said Plott. "I've kept out five hundred head of the mostly young she-stuff that you asked for—that weren't no problem since the buyers mostly want steers, since they're the ones packing the weight."

"Are they the ones in the pens closest to town?" asked Ethan.

"Yep. And if they're what you're lookin' for, they'll cost you twenty dollars a head."

"The same price we agreed on while we were still at Fort Laramie," reminded Collins.

"Since we've already seen the cows I suggest we call it a done deal and get on our way," said Ethan.

"Agreed," said Plott, and then, turning to Cole, he said, "I reckon you'll be wantin' to spend some time at your brother's ranch after you help deliver the cattle, so as soon as he's tired of havin' you around boluxing things up in Wyoming, come on back down to Texas. Your job will be waitin' for you."

"I appreciate that Mr. Plott, but I just hired on with Ethan here, so I reckon I'll be stayin' in Wyoming."

Ethan, Jake, Cole, and three of Plott's cowhands pushed the herd west toward Leantown, and since the idea was to get them to their destination in good shape, the pace that was set was a leisurely one. At night the men weren't worn out and could sit around the campfire and play cards or listen to Jake's tales about the Rocky Mountains.

Ethan used his time to teach his brother how to improve what he laughingly referred to as his "fast draw." Unfortunately, Ethan figured that most of his work with his kid brother was just a waste of time, since it was obvious to anyone with eyes that Cole just didn't have the speed that was necessary to survive a gunfight. His only asset was his ability to shoot accurately. Ethan could see what would end up as an epitaph on his brother's tombstone if he developed a habit of getting into gunfights: "Here lies so and so. He shot straight, but way too slow."

Finally, Ethan came up with a plan that used Cole's ability to shoot straight to overcome his lack of speed. The technique involved his drawing with his right hand and raking the palm of his left hand across the hammer, pulling it back until the hammer was cocked, and then firing from the hip. With his ability to shoot accurately, and if he could get close enough to the other man, there was at least a chance that he could get lead into his opponent before he got poked full of holes himself. Cole had another problem that his brother could do nothing about—he lacked a killer instinct. With a pack of hired killers on his trail, that could end up being a fatal flaw.

Ethan also took the time on their leisurely trip to the fort to write another letter to his father explaining that Cole was now with him, and talking about his plans to start a ranch in Wyoming. It took quite a bit of doing and nagging on his part, but before they reached the fort, Cole would also have a letter to post addressed to his father.

Not being one to waste time, Ethan took the opportunity of their short stay at the fort to buy the grain, seed, and farm implements he would need at the ranch. He also made arrangements to purchase the freight wagons that the implements and grain would be delivered in.

Ethan discovered that a couple of letters had arrived in answer to the ones he had sent out earlier. The one from his father covered pretty much the same information that Cole had already given him. The only new information given in the letter was that Andy Adams had hired Morgan Hawks to see that Cole ended up dead. The second letter came from Taw Skerns in Alaska. It turned out that he liked Ethan's idea and was now packing up and planned to arrive in Leantown as soon as there was a good pack of snow on the ground in Wyoming.

The next day the herd was back on the trail to Leantown, with Ethan making plans to see that everything was in place at his new ranch.

The traveling had been so easy that some of the cattle were actually putting on weight. The cows were content, the cowboys were happy, and Jackson was fairly itching to get back to what he had come to think of as home. Plott's men were looking forward to the extra cash that they would be paid for the drive to Leantown, and Jake was looking forward to playing a part in building a prosperous town in the wilderness.

Cole was feeling safer than he had in many months. Even riding the drag that day couldn't put a damper on his spirits.

When he rode over a hill and came face-to-face with Billy Hanks, though, things started to cloud up a bit for him.

Hanks was smiling as he sidestepped his horse until he was only a few feet from Cole and they were facing each other, side by side. Billy had wanted to take Cole on much earlier but he'd always been around too much law or too close to that blasted brother of his for him to call out. Now he had him in the perfect spot, for as soon as he shot Cole from his saddle he knew the herd would spook, causing a stampede that would keep Ethan and his hired help too busy to check on what the shooting was about.

Hanks figured that there would be plenty of time to lop off Cole's head and stuff it in the sack draped over his saddle horn. Then Adams would have the proof he demanded, and Hanks would have the bounty money. While he figured he would have plenty of time to perform the task, he'd still brought along a hatchet so he could do the job more quickly. The gunman was so confident in his plan, in fact, that he hadn't even bothered to draw his weapon and have it at the ready when Cole came over the hill.

Beginning a leisurely draw, Hanks said, "Boy, you sure are a lot of trouble."

Cole knew two things just then: his life was on the line, and he was way too slow with a gun to go against Hanks. Still, he had no choice. He went for his weapon using what Ethan had taught him. Hanks was surprised that the boy's gun was pointing in his direction, but he still managed to get off the first shot. The second report came from Cole's weapon, and both men fell to the ground where the dry soil soaked up their blood.

As Billy had expected, the gunfire spooked the herd and sent them running in a blind panic. To make matters worse, with the cattle being well fed and rested and not worn out and hungry from traveling miles on sparse graze, they were primed and ready for an all-out run. While it was touch and go for a while, the experienced hands finally got the cattle back under control. Ethan and Jake only ended up losing fifteen head in the stampede, and after things had settled down, Jackson started to ride back in the direction where he thought the shot had come from. That is, if it had been only one shot, for at first he thought it might have been two shots. Riding back to what had been the drag, Ethan came across his brother's pinto running loose and caught it up.

Riding a bit farther, he saw an unfamiliar bay atop a hill not half a mile away. As he came up to the horse he saw two bodies near it at the bottom of the hill. Dismounting, he walked up to the body of his brother. The side of his shirt was bloody, and Ethan could see where he had stuffed dryed grass into the wound to staunch the bleeding. He hadn't been all that successful, and the ground where he had been lying was starting to get soggy from all of the blood that was leaking out of the large wound in his side.

Tearing off a piece of his shirt, Ethan set to making a bandage and, after washing out the wound with water from his canteen, he tightly bound the wound to keep it from bleeding any further.

When Ethan was satisfied that he had done all that he could for Cole, he walked over to Hanks's body. He wanted to further check it over, having already made sure that the man was dead. He noted that the gunman was sporting a very neat .44-caliber hole over his heart. Lifting him onto his bay, Ethan mounted his own horse and rode over to a ravine, where he unceremoniously dumped the body, stripped the saddle from the bay, threw it on top of the gunman's carcass, and covered everything with brush.

It wasn't what a civilized man might call a proper burial, but Ethan wanted to make sure that Cole wasn't given the credit for ending Hanks's career. And while some folks would have felt bad about coyotes dining on Billy's bones, Ethan figured that varmint food was a fitting end for someone who made a career out of murdering what, for the most part, were innocent people.

Cole made the rest of the trip in the back of the chuck wagon which his brother had also purchased from Plott. It was in that wagon that Cole related the story of the gunfight to Ethan and Jake.

"He'd started his draw," Cole began, "and I pretty much figured that I was done for, but then I remembered what you taught me about firing from the hip. So I grabbed my pistol with my right hand and raked back the hammer with the palm of my left like you showed me."

"Did you beat him to the draw?" asked Ethan.

"Almost. I was real surprised about that, but Hanks was the one who really got shook up about it. You should have seen the look on his face when he saw how close I came to beating him to the draw. I reckon that's what caused him to rush his shot. But he still managed to get lead into me first and had just pulled back the hammer to finish me off when I plugged him."

"Dang, if you Jackson boys ain't the luckiest critters I've ever seen. I reckon Limping Dog was right about some folks being looked after by the Great Spirit," said Jake.

"And if you expect the Great Spirit to keep looking after you, little brother, this had better be the last time you tell that story to anybody."

"Why's that?"

" 'Cause Hanks had a reputation as being a top man when it came to using a gun, and since you shot him, you now own that reputation. If you tell that story to anyone else there's going to be more men wanting to nail your hide to the barn door than you have hunting you now—and you've already got plenty after you as it is."

As what his brother had said slowly started to dawn on him, Cole could only shake his head and say, "Not much of a future in that."

"Amen to that. Now you know why I'm looking for a quieter life."

Taking a more direct route to where his ranch house was being built, they bypassed the town with the herd and arrived two days later.

The house was already finished and the barn was almost complete. Kenton and his crew were hard at work at some of the other projects Jackson had asked him to do.

After the introductions were made, Ethan asked Caleb about how things were going in town. Knowing what Jackson was really asking, Kenton told him that Sharon was doing fine.

"How's the mining going?" asked Jake.

"Slowing down quite a bit. I figure that if a good size strike ain't found soon, this is the last year that the town will grow any. Some of the miners have already given up and moved on. I've hired a lot of them who didn't even make themselves enough of a grubstake working the creeks around here to move on." Pausing, Caleb looked around at the work he had done on Ethan's ranch and thought of how many houses he had helped to build in Leantown. After thinking about how much of his time he had invested in the community, he said to Ethan, "I sure hope your plan to save the town works out."

Kenton had the sawmill delivered to Jackson's ranch so he could take advantage of the large number of trees nearby and wouldn't have to haul the finished lumber very far to the many work sites on the property. With as many projects as Ethan had in mind, he figured that he would be busy on the ranch until winter called an end to the building. If more gold wasn't found, though, or Ethan's ranch couldn't provide enough jobs, everything that he and his family had help build in the wilderness would end up being for nothing—it was a fate that he planned to prevent from happening.

Chapter Twelve
Homecoming

Everybody in Leantown who remembered what a beefsteak tasted like had their mouths watering as they watched Ethan and Jake drive several steers down the main street in town.

Sharon and Corey ran out into the street to greet Ethan. Sharon hugged him while Corey stood off to the side to formally shake hands with the man he had begun to think of as his new pa.

"How many head of cattle did you buy?" asked Sharon.

"Five hundred, minus these steers I brought in for your and Jake's restaurant. We talked it over and we figured that there must be plenty of folks around here who are tired of chewing on wild game who would jump at the chance to chow down on a steak from a genuine Texas longhorn."

"I'd bet on that," agreed Sharon. Then, noticing Cole standing behind Ethan, she asked, "Who's that with you, Ethan?"

Turning and hooking his thumb in his younger brother's direction he said, "That's my kid brother, Cole." Then motioning for him to join them, he said, "Cole, this is Sharon O'Brien and her son Corey."

Taking off his hat, Cole walked up beside them and said, "Howdy ma'am." And, since Ethan had told him of his plans to marry Sharon and adopt Corey, he turned to her son and added, "Well, Corey, I reckon that I'm going to be your new uncle."

Corey broke into a smile, stuck out his hand, and said, "Howdy, Uncle Cole."

It was the first time in months that Cole had felt like laughing. Taking an immediate liking to the boy, he began to think that his brother was a whole lot smarter than he'd given him credit for. And he began to think about how nice it would be to settle down some place safe and live among friends and family again.

"Well, pard," he said, addressing Corey, "why don't you show me around town while the old folks here get caught up on the news?"

Happy to have someone around who was closer to his own age for a change, Corey readily agreed to show Cole around town and they walked off together up the street with Corey acting as guide. Jake, knowing that three was a crowd, continued to drive the cattle on to the restaurant where he planned to supervise the preparation of that night's supper. He knew that the eatery would be getting mighty crowded as soon as word got out that beefsteaks were on the menu.

Business had been so good at the store that Sharon had been able to hire a clerk. This gave her some free time, which she now used to join Ethan at the restaurant. He drank coffee while she told him of recent events that had occurred in and around town during the last few months.

"John Baldwin's still keeping the peace and there's not been any real trouble around town to speak of, but there's been some things going on politically around town that's got me worried," she said, as she refilled his coffee cup.

Being the type of man who believed in getting to the point, he asked, "What's the problem?"

"Well, as you know, there's always been arguments about how things are run around town among some of those folks who came here on the wagon train last year."

"Yeah."

"Well, the worst of the bunch is a man who Jake brought back from that bunch of fools who tried to go through the pass after it was snowed in last year. His name is Aaron Brown, and the group he's sort of the leader of has been grousing about how the town is being run; especially about the miners passing through town not having any say."

The coffee was too weak for his taste, but Ethan was much too interested in what Sharon was saying for him to take the time to make a fresh pot for himself.

"That bunch didn't strike me as being too concerned about what was fair or not. And they certainly didn't appear to be interested in the principles of democracy. As far as the miners are concerned, I doubt that they would even allow a miner inside their homes if he were freezin' or starvin' to death."

"That's the way most everybody else sees it," she said.

"Then why their interest in the poor miner?"

"The way I see it is that they want to use the miners' votes to get control of the town council, put their people in charge, and start taxing everybody within the city limits."

Ethan thought about what she said and it made sense. After all, everybody was looking for some way to get their hands on the gold that was being found. The miner tried to get it with a pick and a shovel; the gambler with his deck of cards; now, the politicians had arrived with their taxes. Looking out the window at the street, he began thinking about what would happen to the town he desperately wanted to settle in if the group of men who had shown so little judgement were to get hold of the reins of the town council. When he thought of the damage they could end up doing, the thoughts of taxes that they might levy didn't seem so bad compared to the other things they might do when it came to making laws.

"Has it occurred to anybody that those people that Jake risked his life to dig out of the snow didn't bring a thing to the town? They had to leave their wagons and gear in the mountains when they were rescued, and the animals that they hadn't eaten to stay alive died on the trail back here. If it hadn't been for the folks taking them in that winter, they would have all died of exposure and starvation. I think it's pretty nervy of a bunch of yahoos who ain't nothing more than guests in the community telling us how to run it. Why don't the town council just tell them to git?"

"Because the membership of the town council has changed since you left."

"How'd it change?"

"A man was elected to fill Jake's position after he left with you and the Kentons. And it was during this election that it was decided that everybody should be allowed to vote—including the miners."

"Who won?"

"Jim Cooper."

Ethan was glad that he had set his cup of coffee on the table, for if he'd been drinking it at the time he would have probably choked.

"Have the folks around here lost their minds? I've seen chickens that have shown more sense than that loud-mouthed idiot."

"That's not the worst of it," said Sharon.

Ethan hated to ask, but he knew that sooner or later he would find out what could be worse than having someone as dumb as Cooper being on the town council, so he asked, "What could be worse than what you've already told me?"

"It seems that folks have decided that a third member is needed to break up any tie votes that come up during council meetings."

"But that's what Emitt Lawson did as mayor."

"I know, but the new council member is calling for the mayor's duties to be more along the lines of running the day-to-day business of the town."

It was right then that Ethan was beginning to wonder if the citizens of Leantown had ever heard of the expression: "If it ain't broke, don't fix it." He wondered what kind of a person they would pick to run in double harness with somebody like Cooper.

"Who they got in mind for the third council member?"

Sharon was uncomfortable and hesitated before she spoke. "Lonnie Leary."

After hearing that, Ethan didn't trust himself to say much of anything without resorting to cursing, so he held his tongue. He spent the rest of the morning ignoring the subject and only spoke of more pleasant things—mostly of his plans for the ranch.

That afternoon Jackson dropped in on Baldwin and was surprised at how easily the fairly new lawman had adopted the mannerisms of an experienced sheriff. Joining him on his rounds that evening, Ethan noticed how the sheriff scanned the street, looking twice at anything that seemed the least bit out of place, his eyes in constant motion, taking in everything. There was no doubt that Baldwin was a fast learner.

"How's the job going?" Ethan asked.

"Fine. I'm getting used to it and it seems natural."

"Thinking about maybe doing it permanently?"

"Like to. But I'm not too sure about how long I'll be

keeping the job with the new town council doing the hiring and firing. And if Lonnie Leary gets elected, I'm sure of two things: he will start pushing to get me fired, and I wouldn't even think of having him for a boss."

Remembering his own reaction to the news of the possibility of Leary's election, Jackson said, "Understandable."

"I just hate the idea of having this town we've all worked so hard to keep going being run by a bunch of fools," said Baldwin.

"So do I," agreed Ethan, "but short of shooting all of them, I don't see what we can do about it. We can't just take over and say the law doesn't matter—we're the ones who put the law in charge; how can we just up and chuck it out when it doesn't suit us?"

Nodding his head in agreement, Baldwin pushed open the doors of the Gold Star Saloon and they walked in. Picking a table in the back of the room, they walked over and sat down. They then both ordered beers from the bartender who came over to their table.

Taking out a slip of paper, Ethan asked the girl who brought them their drinks if the saloon had a bulletin board. When she said they did, he handed her the paper and asked her to post the note.

On the slip of paper he had written that he was looking to hire five cattle hands to work his ranch. With that out of the way, he turned to John and asked, "What's your plans if Leary does get on the town council?"

"I suppose I'll try to do here what I planned on doing in Oregon—farming."

"Mighty short growing season for crops at this altitude," observed Jackson.

"Not for potatoes," said Baldwin. "There's some mighty rich soil a bit lower down that ought to produce some mighty fine spuds. And there's always chickens. Up in

Maine and Rhode Island they've developed some hardy and heavy breeds of poultry that should be able to survive our winters."

"I like your ideas, John. As a matter of fact, they fit right into some of the plans I've been working on."

"How's that?"

"You're going to need some way to ship those potatoes to market, and I plan to use the wagons I've bought to start a freight line between here and the rail line in Cheyenne," said Jackson.

John thought about what had been said and then replied, "Looks like you've been giving the matter plenty of thought."

"You know what it's like up here in the winter: not a whole lot to do other than think, plan, and eat. And it was a long winter last year."

"I suppose," said John, "but that brings up another problem we're going to have when it comes to getting folks to settle here—the isolation that winter brings with it."

"Yep. There's no doubt about how isolated we are up here after the first big snow hits, but I may even have a solution for that."

"What do you mean?"

"I don't want to say until I'm pretty sure it's going to work. So I'll just keep it under my hat for now."

Baldwin was plenty curious about what his friend might be planning, but he didn't push for an answer. He had just taken notice of three men walking toward his and Ethan's table.

Facing Ethan and John, the man in the lead spoke first. "One of you gents called Ethan Jackson?"

Ethan had also become alert when he noticed the three men moving in his direction, but he quickly relaxed when he saw their deeply tanned faces and noticed the bowlegged gait with which they all walked—they were cowboys, not gunmen.

"I'm Jackson," said Ethan. "What can I do for you?"

The apparent leader of the group spoke again. "My name's Red Adkins, and this is George Klauss and Marcus Krebbs," he said, indicating the two men beside him.

"Howdy," said Ethan.

"I just read the notice that you posted about wanting to hire on some cowhands. Well, before me and my two compadres here got bit by the gold bug, we were pretty fair hands with a rope back in Colorado."

They all looked to be somewhere in their mid-twenties and had the look of good-natured hands who knew when to fight and when to ride easy, so Ethan asked, "You working steady before you came here?"

"Sure was," said Adkins. "Had good jobs, every one of us on a big ranch. I reckon we all went a little crazy when we heard about gold being found here and we just had to run off and ride to here and start panning for gold."

"How come you don't just go back to Colorado?" asked Jackson.

"Because the man who owned the outfit told us that if we left he'd have to hire men to replace us and he wasn't going to fire good men so we could have our jobs back. Not that we blame him for that—we'd feel the same way if the shoe was on the other foot and some muddle-headed cowboys came back wanting the jobs we'd signed on for. But being that there ain't no shortage of cowboys in Colorado right now, we figured the smartest thing we can do is to take a job wherever we can find it; it beats asking ranchers to feed us on the grub line."

Having ridden the grub line a time or two himself, Jackson agreed with Red's logic. "Seems reasonable," said Ethan. "And I need the help. Pay's thirty a month and found, but I think that I ought to tell you right off that you ain't going to be riding into no paradise if you come to work for me. Not that I figure I'm all that hard to work for or anything. All I ask for is a day's work for a day's pay. The hard part comes from the fact that you may have to use those pistols you're packing."

"Against who?" asked Adkins.

"Have you heard of me before?"

"We know your reputation, Mr. Jackson," answered Red.

"Well, there's always the chance that somebody, usually some kid, will show up looking to take me on. This has happened plenty of times before, and believe me boys, it gets real tiresome. I've been trying to avoid gunfights for quite awhile in hopes of shedding this reputation I've been saddled with and so far I've been real lucky at not having to add to it. Mostly thanks to the sheriff here keeping a tight lid on the town when it comes to gunfights. And it's my intention to run pretty much the same type of operation out at my ranch. By that I mean to keep peace out there the same way John keeps it here by hiring men who aren't gunfighters but who do know how to use a sidearm and when to draw it. Basically what I'll be wanting you to do is to run off anybody coming around hunting trouble. So I'm not looking for somebody to fight my battles for me, just some men with enough guts to keep the peace on the ranch."

Waiting a few seconds for what he'd said to sink in, he then added, "One more thing you should know before you decide to sign on. I've got a kid brother who got into a scrape back in Ohio and managed to make somebody real mad. It's all ended with that man hiring somebody to kill him, and since he's going to be living with us out at the ranch there's a real good chance that some hired killers will show up out there sooner or later."

"What's the name of the man who's been hired to kill your brother?" asked Red.

"Morgan Hawks."

Whistling low, Red said, "Your brother must have made that feller back in Ohio real mad. I hear that Hawks is real expensive—and good at his job."

"That's right," said Ethan. "Now that you know how things stand around here you can change your minds about coming to work for me. I won't be thinking hard of you if you decide to head back to Colorado or somewhere else to look for work. Matter of fact, I'd think of you boys as being downright smart if you decided to pull out."

They all huddled together for a few seconds and then Red said, "None of us have ever been accused of being particularly smart, so I reckon we'll be takin' those jobs you're offerin'."

Shaking hands with all of them to seal the deal, Jackson said, "You boys can ride out with the supply wagon over at the general store." And then, figuring that his new hands were probably broke, especially after eating and drinking for awhile at mining town prices, he dug into his poke and counted out thirty silver dollars and laid them on the table in front of the men, saying, "Sign on bonus of ten dollars each. Get whatever business you need to get done in town and be ready to ride for the ranch in about an hour."

To broke men ten dollars could look as big as a wagon wheel, and to Red and his friends just then that was what that silver on the table looked like. Each man scooped up the windfall, thanked their new boss, and walked across the street to have their first meal in two days. They hadn't found any gold and until just then, the only luck they had been having was all bad.

"They're good boys," said Baldwin. "They've been here

for the better part of a month looking for gold but they never found any."

"Any trouble with them?"

"No. They're good, hard-working men. You picked well."

Chapter Thirteen
Politics

Aaron Brown had been agitating for another council member, and Lonnie Leary had been his choice to fill the office. Not because he considered him to be the best man for the job, but because he could easily be controlled. Unfortunately, while he could have been easily bought and told how to vote on the issues, he wouldn't have been all that easy to get elected, for a good number of the voters—including the miners—had gotten to know Leary from his bullying around town, and on his best day, Lonnie wasn't the kind of man who made friends—a necessary skill for a politician. Just about the only influence he exercised among the people was a result of his size and strength. So Brown decided to run for the office himself. He could always use Lonnie in an appointed office—maybe as sheriff.

Brown wasn't going to find getting himself elected to be all that easy, however, for word had spread about how he had led a group of people into the mountains and almost got them all killed. It was a sure thing that none of those who followed him into the mountains last year would be casting a vote for him. He knew it would be quite a battle getting elected. But then again, it wasn't like he hadn't gotten someone unpopular elected to office before, for with the help of the owner of the Gold Star Saloon, Alphonse Wright, he had pushed Jim Cooper into office. It was the money and whiskey that flowed into the campaign coffers that got Cooper elected, and Wright had agreed to finance Aaron's campaign in the same manner. Of course, Wright expected to be left alone to run his saloon as he saw fit after Brown's people were sitting on the town council.

Leantown had pretty much split into two camps, with the members of each faction becoming almost rabid in their support of their candidate. All of the original settlers, and almost all of the people who had arrived on the wagon trains, were supporting Jake Collins, who was trying to re-gain his seat on the council. The other faction was made up of men such as Wright and some of the gamblers, who were fighting for Aaron's election so they could ply their trade without interference from the law. The wild card in the election was the miners, but it was expected that they would vote for Brown since many of them remembered, and those who hadn't been there at the time were told, about how it had been Jake's faction who had denied the miners the vote during the first election.

The two weeks before the election were filled with plenty of politicking, and while there was no formal speechmaking going on, there were plenty of lively discussions taking place among the members of the two factions, with more than one fist-fight breaking out among the participants. On the Brown side, money and whiskey flowed in almost equal amounts, while the supporters of Collins tried talking to persuade the miners to support their candidate.

On the day of the election, Jake, after watching the voters file in and out of the polling booth for a good part of the day, pronounced himself the loser of the election. He felt he had made a fairly good tally in his head.

"How'd you know that?" asked Cole Jackson, who was enjoying the excitement of the election which he considered to be much more colorful than the ones he'd seen back in Ohio; back there the voters didn't show up wearing pistols and spurs.

"Son, all you have to do is take a look at the ones going through who seem like they're nursing a hangover or look like they can't wait to get started on a drunk and you can figure that there goes another vote for Aaron Brown. And the way I see it, a whole lot more of his supporters are showing up than mine."

As things turned out, Collins would once again prove that he had a real head for figures. When the final count was made, Jake lost 420 to 97.

Brown didn't waste any time putting his plan to work. That night Baldwin and his deputies each received notice that their services were no longer required, and they were ordered to surrender their badges to the newly appointed sheriff—Lonnie Leary.

Lonnie, who had been arrested several times for brawling by John and his deputies, enjoyed delivering those notices to each of the lawmen in person. He especially enjoyed handing the notice to Baldwin at his home that evening. Smirking as John handed the badge over to him, Leary pinned it to his own chest and said, "Well, schoolteacher, looks like your skinny butt's out of a job. What do you think of that?"

"Leary, has it ever occurred to you that a man can only be pushed as far as he's willing to be pushed?"

"Huh? What's that mean?"

"I'll make it real simple for you, Leary," Baldwin said as he pulled the skirt of his coat back to reveal the Colt he always carried in his waistband. "I'm not inclined to be pushed tonight. You got anything else you want to say?"

Knowing that he'd pushed his luck as far as he dared to that night, Lonnie turned and walked away without saying another word.

That fall Leantown turned into two distinct communities, with most of the decent folks congregating around the O'Brien general store, and the Brown faction staying close to the Gold Star Saloon. The saloon had turned into what a preacher would have called a den of iniquity, where a knifing or a shooting was something that occurred on a regular basis.

Cooper and Brown were running the town council and ignoring the mayor. And since they were in the majority in the council, Phillip Jenkins was helpless when it came to preventing Brown and Cooper from making up whatever laws they cared to pass.

Finally, seeing the futility of their positions, Jenkins and the mayor stopped showing up for regularly scheduled meetings. That left only Cooper and Brown to run the town. In truth, Aaron Brown was the only one left to run the town, for he had found Cooper to be almost useless for even the most menial tasks and had dismissed him and hired other men more capable of doing what had to be done.

Cooper griped and complained to anyone who would listen, but he failed to find anybody who cared about his plight; most of them—including his wife—figured he had got what he deserved.

Lonnie Leary was town sheriff in name only. He spent most of his time in the Gold Star or in one of his own jail cells sleeping off another drunk. He wasn't even able to act as a jailer most of the time because of his fondness for the bottle. But Brown might need him for something official sometime, so he hired a man to act as jailer to not only lock up the miners who needed somewhere to sleep off a night's celebrating, but to also watch over Leary and see to it that the sheriff didn't throw up and drown in his own vomit. Leary's wife was no longer available for that job, since she had left him and taken a job working in Miss O'Brien's restaurant.

As to keeping law and order in town, everybody was pretty much on their own. Each man took to keeping a gun handy at his place of business or home. The more well-to-do hired guards; Baldwin's deputies found work doing that very thing. John used his new freedom from a regular job to start a school for the few children in the community.

The Jacksons and Jake Collins spent most of their time out at the ranch, where they worked to get things ready for winter. Before the snow hit they had the barn filled with hay and grain, the shelters built for the cattle, and enough firewood cut to make sure that they wouldn't have to break out an axe until spring.

The freight line Ethan had started was kept busy through the fall shipping in supplies to his ranch and Leantown, the result being that both the community and his ranch were now ready to batten down the hatches and prepare for a long period of isolation from the outside world.

At least that was what everybody expected. Then, three days after the first heavy snow, a strange sound could be heard in the air. It was barking—not the type heard from a farm dog guarding the homeplace, but the voices of many dogs. They seemed to be coming from above the valley.

Throwing a final fork full of hay to his horse, Ethan climbed down from the loft of the barn and walked outside. Suddenly, he caught sight of a dog-sled team top the rise, float over the deep snow into the valley, and head for his barn. Jackson was smiling when the team stopped beside him. Climbing out of the furs he had burrowed into came Ethan's old friend, Taw Skerns.

"Surprised that somebody ain't hung you yet," said Skerns as he stepped off the sled and set the brake.

Grasping his old friend's hand, Ethan said, "I could always smell the oil when they started in to greasin' the hangin' rope, and got out of town before they could find me."

Laughing, Taw said, "Well, old son, I'm here. Your letter said that you might have a job for me this winter. That still the way the wind's blowin'?"

"Yep. Come on in and let's talk it over."

Taw Skerns had grown up in eastern Kentucky where he'd always run hounds after bears, coons, fox, and whatever else gave him and his dogs a chance to chase it. Along with his love of the chase came a strong urge to see what was on the other side of the hill. It wasn't that he wanted to see if the grass was greener on the other side so much as he just wanted to see what was on the other side.

With a talent for working with dogs and an itchy foot that led him to Alaska, it was only natural that he would take to driving a dog team. He also liked to tell folks about what life was like in Alaska for a man who made his living doing that very thing. During those long nights in a cabin he had gotten into the habit of putting pen to paper and telling everybody he could think of about his experiences driving dogs in the winter. That was how Ethan had first found out about what a dog-sled team could do—he'd been the recipient of one of the letters penned by Taw five years earlier. The story that Skerns had related in the letter had been fascinating, and Ethan had read it so many times that he had destroyed it through folding and unfolding the paper. But he remembered enough of what his friend had written to spark the idea that he was now pitching to Skerns.

Taking the coffee that Ethan offered him, Taw said, "Your letter said you wanted to open up a winter freight line in the mountains. You still planning on doing that?"

"Yep," answered Jackson. "How much weight you figure you can haul on the sled outside?"

"Oh, around half a ton; more if I have to."

"Did you bring another team like I asked?"

"Sure did. I left them in Cheyenne with the other sled. You got somebody to drive the other team?"

"Two drivers, as a matter of fact."

"They got much experience with dogs?"

Looking a bit uncomfortable, Ethan said, "Not exactly."

"How much is not exactly?" pressed Skerns.

"None."

Laughing, Taw asked, "These old boys got names?"

"Yeah. You know one of them real well . . . me."

Spilling some of the coffee he was drinking into his lap, Taw said, "I reckon the other driver is your pa . . . or ma."

"Not exactly," he said sheepishly. "It's my brother, Cole."

"Keepin' it in the family ain't ya?"

"Sort of," agreed Jackson. "I know we don't have the experience, but we're both fast learners and neither one of us likes being cooped up in the winter. I figure that running a team of dogs through the mountains ought to keep us from getting cabin fever."

"Oh, ridin' trail in winter can keep you occupied all right. You'll spend most of your time trying to keep from freezing to death out in the open; not to mention dealing with hungry wolves and cougars who'll be sharing the trail with you. As a matter of fact, I had a cougar and some Indians watching me from the hills."

Remembering his experience with Limping Dog, Ethan said, "Yeah, we got some real curious critters around here all right; some of them walk on four legs—others walk on two. You'll get used to seeing them around. You willing to give my idea a try?"

"I reckon, but I ain't turnin' you or your brother loose with my dogs 'till I'm satisfied that both of you know how to run 'em."

"Fair enough," said Jackson.

The rest of the week Taw Skerns took on the role of teacher while Ethan and Cole became eager students determined to learn how to pilot a team of huskies over the snow. Both Jacksons proved to be able pupils and had soon become good enough with the dogs to be allowed to drive them on their own.

Ethan had put out the word that he would be providing mail service between Leantown and Cheyenne where the letters would be put on a train headed for other parts of the country. He had also been right about how the other isolated communities at the higher elevations would want to use his freighting and mail service. Eager people starved for information about what was going on outside of their own little towns grabbed at newspapers he carried. It was to those locations that Ethan had taken to dispatching his little brother so that he wouldn't be running into any of Adams's hired killers.

Ethan kept the more populated settlements where hired guns were likely to show up for either Skerns, or, on occasion, himself. Not that he had all that much time to make such trips, since he had his hands full with supervising the running of his ranch in the valley. Jake helped quite a bit, but he also had his own enterprises to look after, having not only bought an interest in Sharon's restaurant but also invested in several other businesses around town. When one of the better-educated citizens told Collins that a man who did what he was doing was often referred to as an entrepreneur, he laughed and told him that he wasn't inclined to lay claim to being something he couldn't even come close to spelling.

Fewer and fewer people had been finding gold as winter started to gain a stranglehold on Leantown. Word soon spread and when the snow began to get deep no one showed up on skis or snowshoes carrying backpacks as they had the year before. It was beginning to dawn on even the most blinded with gold fever that the gold rush was over, and the only people who would be showing up in Leantown come spring would be those who were passing through on their way to somewhere farther west.

Everybody who had begun to think of Leantown as their home was beginning to worry about whether or not the town could survive without gold. The more industrious among them began to support any effort that was designed to help the town grow and prosper. Everybody who started a new business was treated like royalty, with every citizen doing what he could to make the enterprise a success. As for the miners, most of them were being replaced with men who were willing to work regular hours for regular pay and couldn't wait to get out of town. A steady stream of passengers developed that kept Ethan and Skerns busy ferrying them to Cheyenne three to six passengers at a time. The traffic became so steady that on occasion the transportation of mail had to be curtailed to permit more passengers.

Aaron Brown was happy to see the businesses succeed, for that meant he could tax them and send out his henchmen to collect what was due. When asked about when he planned to use some of that money he was collecting to make improvements around town, Brown would say that he was waiting for spring when the weather would permit public works to be done. In truth, all of the money that was being collected—minus what he paid to his henchmen—was ending up in a safe in Aaron's office, where he planned to take off with it as soon as he figured he had collected as much of it as he could get away with or until his base of support, the miners, were gone.

He had started out to take over the town because of his pride and to get over his embarrassment of leading a party of his friends into the mountains where they almost died. That motive had rapidly changed to pure greed when he began to take notice of the amount of tax money flowing into the town coffers. It was then he decided to drain Lean-town of as much of its wealth as he could, abandon his wife and children, and head for a big city somewhere back east where he could parlay the money he was stealing into a fortune and live the kind of life a man like him was meant to live.

Brown could see that he was losing his power base with the miners leaving at such a rapid pace, and he knew that it wouldn't be long before Ethan Jackson and his friends would be back in power. Even Alphonse Wright and the denizens of the Gold Star Saloon were getting ready to pack their bags and head for more fertile ground to ply their trade. Aaron figured the best he could do was to keep on collecting taxes from the sheep in town and then ride on out as soon as the weather broke. If things got too hot for him he could always buy passage on Jackson's dog-sled freight line—the thought of doing that really amused him for some reason.

Sharon's and Jake's businesses were the ones proving to be the most profitable in town and were therefore the ones suffering the most from Brown's taxes. And they were none too happy with the councilman's accounting practices. It would be the practices of Brown's tax collectors, though, that would light the fuse that would cause everything to blow up in Brown's face. Sensing that the good times of easy picking were about to come to an end, the henchmen began to get bolder in their demands for money and began lining their own pockets by stealing from the merchants. It was that indiscretion that would cause Aaron's gravy train to come to a halt.

Brown had hired three lumbering oafs to do his tax collecting for him. He had hired them for attributes or talents that he had a use for. The first was physical, with each man standing several inches over six feet tall. The second trait they shared was a talent for following orders without asking questions. The third and most important trait they shared was their willingness to do as they were told with a complete lack of conscience as long as they were being paid enough money.

Unfortunately, they lacked good judgement the day they reached into Sharon's cash register and started scooping up bank notes and stuffing them into their pockets.

"Put it back," ordered Jackson, who'd just witnessed their brazen thievery.

The three tax collectors were used to getting their way. Usually just towering over whoever was foolish enough to complain about their collection methods had been enough to stifle any protests from the citizens—up until then.

While they weren't what could be called the sharpest tools in the shed, they did realize that they weren't dealing with just another merchant, but with a man who had killed more than his fair share of men and who was now bracing them with his gunhand resting near his Colt.

Then one of the men named Fred Porter remembered something that Brown had once told him. While Jackson was deadly with a gun, he had been trying to live down his reputation. And that if Fred ever had any trouble with him he was to make sure that he and the rest of the collectors got rid of their pistols and forced Jackson into a brawl where the three of them would have the advantage over the lone man.

"Hold on, Jackson," said Porter, holding out his hands. Then, looking at his companions, he said, "Unbuckle your gunbelts and let 'em drop."

The other two men looked at each other in confusion, and when they didn't do as Porter had ordered, he said, "Drop 'em now!"

Not knowing what Porter was up to, but being well aware of what Jackson could do with a pistol, they unbuckled their weapons and let them drop to the floor.

Fred then kicked his own dropped weapon toward the door and said, "All right, boys, kick your guns as far away from you as you can."

Obliging Porter, who had taken on the job as leader of the outfit, they also kicked their weapons toward the door.

Jackson was more than a little confused by their actions. They hardly seemed the type who could use their heads. Oh, of course, he had them pegged as cowards, but every coward that he'd ever seen in his life had to bluster some before he backed down and ran off with his tail tucked between his legs. These thugs, however, were showing good judgement by not trying to brace him—it alerted him to the point where the tiny hairs on the back of his neck stood up.

Ethan wasn't confused for very long about what they were up to. "All right, Jackson," said Porter. "We're unarmed and we ain't puttin' one cent back into the till. What you goin' to do about that?"

So that was it. They knew that them being unarmed meant that he couldn't use his gun on them without being tried, and probably convicted, of murder. On the other hand, if he tried to take on three men by himself he'd probably end up being kicked to death, for he knew that with three-to-one odds there was a good chance that he would go down. And then there was Sharon and Corey to think about, for after he was beaten to death, the three men wouldn't want two witnesses left to tell how it happened.

Before he let that happen, there would be three dead men on the floor bleeding from the .45-caliber holes he would put in them. A jury would find him guilty of murder, but two people he cared deeply about would be safe. And then a plan formed in his mind. Without taking his eyes off of the three men in front of him, Ethan said, "Sharon, you and Corey take those guns they shucked and go find Baldwin."

Seeing that Porter was about to protest Sharon's leaving, Jackson drew his revolver, eared back the hammer, and said, "Friend, if you or any of the others try to stop her from leaving, I start shooting, and while I won't be shooting to kill, I do plan on tearing you up so bad that the only job you'll ever be able to get is swamping out a saloon."

Taking Ethan at his word, they all backed away to allow Sharon and her son to pass by. After they were safely out of the way, Jackson holstered his gun, took off his hat, walked up to Porter and said, "Remember, you asked for this." He then slapped Fred across his face with his stetson. Swiftly stepping backwards, he kicked out with the toe of his boot and struck Porter in an area where no man wanted to be kicked, which caused Fred to drop to the floor moaning in pain. Sidestepping to the right, Ethan jabbed a left hook into the stomach of the second tax collector who doubled up, and when he turned his head sideways to look at Jackson, Ethan smashed down with a rock-hard fist to the temple that immediately put the thug to sleep.

It was then that Ethan felt the wind rush from his lungs as an axe handle smashed into his stomach causing him to double over. Before he could throw up his arm to block the next blow, the third man brought down the club with such force that it broke in two as it landed on Jackson's back and almost knocked him senseless.

Having lost his weapon, Ethan's opponent resorted to kicking him in the ribs until he noticed that Jackson's pistol was still in its holster. Reaching down, the third thug took the revolver from the holster, leveled it at Ethan's head, and said, "Looks like you lost the draw, gunfighter."

"Won't do you any good, friend," gasped Jackson.

"What?"

"I emptied that gun before the fight started in case one of you got hold of it," said Jackson, pointing to the front of the gun's cylinder. "Look at the cylinder and you'll see that there ain't any bullets in the gun."

The tax collector could have just pulled the trigger while the barrel was still pointing at Ethan's head to see if he was telling the truth—that would have been the smart thing to do. He hadn't been hired for his ability to think, however, but for his willingness to listen to what someone else told him to do. Following his usual habits, he turned up the barrel to look at the cylinder, giving Jackson the opportunity to kick out and strike him behind the knee, which caused the tax collector to drop to the floor, discharging his weapon into the ceiling.

This time the wind was knocked out of the thug, giving Ethan the chance to retrieve his pistol, stick it in the tax collector's ear, and say, "Just in case you haven't figured it out yet, the gun is loaded."

"You lied," said the thug.

"You bet I did," answered Jackson. "It's not the first time I've saved my hide by lying and depending on someone else's curiosity. Now, I tell you what you're going to do to keep from getting into any more trouble: you just lay real still until somebody shows up to put you in jail."

The third man was fuming but he kept his mouth shut and waited until Baldwin and some other men showed up to help Ethan escort his prisoners to the jail. When Leary and the jailer were told about what had happened Lonnie started blustering and protesting that he was the only man in town who was authorized to arrest anybody and that he'd be the one who decided about whether or not someone ended up behind bars. Jackson was tired, bruised, and more than a little put out with Leary, so he got nose-to-nose with the sheriff and told him that he could either jail the prisoners he and Baldwin had brought in and guard them, or he could join them behind bars.

Seeing that Jackson was in no mood to argue, Leary agreed that the men should be confined before their trial. As Jackson was leaving, he turned to Lonnie and said, "And, Leary, if they happen to escape I plan to hold you personally responsible." He then turned and walked out the door with Baldwin.

That evening there was a private meeting in Sharon's store among Kenton, Jackson, Baldwin, Collins, Emitt Lawson, and Councilman Phillip Jenkins about what to do to regain control of the town council.

Lawson was the first to offer an opinion. "There's no point in calling for a new election," he said. "There's still too many miners around who will support Brown."

"We don't need an election to take over the government," offered Collins.

"I know you'd like to just walk in and hang Brown right off," said Ethan, "but we've all worked too hard to establish law in Leantown and I'm not inclined to throw that all away."

"Well, we weren't exactly all that legal about how we started the town council," said Jenkins.

"I'll admit that we cut corners, but we didn't have a choice back then," said Ethan.

"I'm not talking about doing anything illegal," said Jake. "I'm talking about doin' some persuadin' when it comes to a certain member of the council. Namely, Jim Cooper."

"What do you want with that loudmouthed, spineless weasel?" asked Caleb.

"You just laid out what we want him for," said Jake.

Thinking for a few seconds, Kenton said, "Oh, the persuadin' part, I think I know what you're talkin' about. If we can get Cooper to go along with Jenkins here on how to vote, Brown's vote won't amount to a hill of beans."

"You got it," said Jake.

After working out a plan on how to persuade Cooper into joining Jenkins in taking over the council, the meeting adjourned. Before the meeting broke up, it was decided that Kenton should be the one to present their plan to Cooper. Cooper would prove to be agreeable to their proposal, partly because he wanted to get even with Brown for the way he had treated him, and partly because while Caleb had been making the offer he had been sharpening his skinning knife on a whetstone and glancing at Cooper's scalp.

The next town council meeting was scheduled for the next Tuesday. The result of that meeting was to turn everything in Leantown completely around in the matter of one day. Brown was in effect out of office and the tax money he had collected was confiscated and locked away in the sheriff's safe—after Leary had been fired, so the money would be secure. It would be tapped for the funds necessary to make civic improvements and pay the salaries of Baldwin and his deputies, who had once again been hired to patrol the streets of the town. The Gold Star Saloon immediately became a reasonably safe place again where the miners could go to have a drink and play an honest game.

The three men who had collected Brown's taxes for him were given free rides on one of the dog sleds and presented with train tickets for parts outside of the Wyoming territory.

Things settled down around town, and even though winter had wrestled its way in, the town stayed well supplied and had communication with the outside world through newspapers and letters from family members living in other parts of the country, thanks to the sled dogs of Taw Skerns.

The winter was bad but the precautions that Jackson had taken to protect his cattle had paid off; his cows were dropping calves that were surviving at a rate unheard of in that part of the country. Things were looking so prosperous that he and Sharon were planning on being married in the spring and had begun arguing about where they were going to live—in town or out at the ranch. Ethan pretended to hate the idea of living in town and had only reluctantly agreed to live in town because it was what Sharon wanted. Actually, Ethan, having spent a good part of his life living in towns when he worked as a sheriff, had no problem living in a town, but he felt it would be to his advantage to start the marriage off appearing to give in on something so he could argue for something he wanted the next time. Besides, his younger brother had settled in real nice at the ranch. He'd complained at first about how he'd grown to hate cattle, but once he realized that on a ranch he could sleep in his own bed at night, he decided that nursemaiding a bunch of cows wasn't really all that bad of a job. Since he had started courting Caleb Kenton's seventeen-year old daughter the fact that he could go into town almost any time he wanted to was a pretty important benefit when it came to working for his brother.

All things considered, Ethan figured that things were working out fine. But things were about to change—and not for the better.

Chapter Fourteen
The Reckoning

By summer the gold rush in Leantown was over. People still came looking for the yellow ore. A few lucky ones found small amounts of the heavy metal, but most of them ended up leaving town with less money than they brought into the community. A few, seeing that the town had potential, took jobs around town or started working for the "Kenton and Sons Construction Company." A few of the new arrivals took riding jobs on Jackson's ranch, whose brand was a circle RV, which Ethan said stood for Resurrection Valley. It represented his life, for he figured that Sheriff Ethan Jackson had died somewhere along the trail from Missouri and Rancher Ethan Jackson had been reborn in Leantown, Wyoming.

Despite the end of the gold rush, business was booming in the community. Some people were planting potatoes while others were starting up small cattle outfits. Buildings were still going up so fast that Kenton and his boys were being kept busy from daylight to dark at the sawmill filling orders. And there were plenty of jobs available for anybody who wanted them. The gold was gone but the stimulus it had provided was replaced by a spirit of enterprise that had been started by Jackson's cattle operation. It caused almost everyone in the community to look for ways to help the town grow.

Some of the people had even found deposits of coal and were heating their homes with it. A geologist who had come looking for gold had speculated that there was a seam of what he liked to call "Black Gold" running near the outskirts of town that a commercial mining operation might be interested in developing. Along with the coal mining there was the possibility of of iron smelting which would bring good high-paying jobs to the community that would be permanent.

Ethan reflected on how the town he had first sighted two years earlier had grown from a dying community to a prosperous town with the start of nothing more than a story that he and Jake had hatched to hide the location of a gold mine in the Big Horn Mountains. It wasn't just the prosperity of the town that Ethan was happy with, but with the job Baldwin had done keeping the peace in town. It not only made it safe for the average citizen to walk down the street, but also allowed him to keep his gun in his holster, since every would-be gunslinger who arrived in town soon found himself in jail until John figured they had learned that gunslingers weren't welcome in the community.

He was also happy because of the news that he had received from his father telling him that Andy Adams was in ill health and was more occupied with trying to save his own life than trying to end Cole's. Cole could finally begin to enjoy life without having to constantly look over his shoulder for hired killers.

Things were going along so smoothly that Ethan and Sharon had decided that they should get married in June. That was the reason Jackson was riding his horse back from

Cheyenne that afternoon. That spring he had ridden out to one of the streams that had been abandoned by the miners and panned out enough of the gold missed by the rushing prospectors for a jeweler to fashion two wedding bands. Ethan figured that it was only fitting that they should make their bands from the gold that had not only saved the town but had enabled them to stay together in the community. He had taken the gold to a jeweler in Cheyenne who had fashioned the rings into a design he was sure that Sharon would like. He was also sure that she would appreciate the sentiment that went into the bands.

Such were his thoughts as he rode back to Leantown that day and he thus failed to notice the large dust cloud behind him being raised by a party of hard-riding men. Fortunately, he did hear them in time to ride behind a stand of trees and melt into the shadows just before they galloped past him. Jackson didn't recognize any of the faces of the men who rode by, but he did recognize them for what they were—professional gunmen. And they were headed in the direction of Leantown.

Jackson rode fast enough to stay with them but not fast enough to overtake them. It was his goal to arrive in town as close behind them as possible where he would have the advantage of surprise, for while he didn't know why they were riding for Leantown, he was sure that it wasn't for the benefit of anyone living there.

Ethan halted above the valley and watched as the men rode up to the sheriff's office. Jackson watched as Baldwin and one of his deputies walked out to meet them. They were much too far away for Ethan to hear what was said but he could sense that trouble was about to start. Sure enough, the two riders in front wheeled their horses to the left and the right and the men behind them started shooting. Both Baldwin and his deputy went down under the withering fire, but not before John emptied two saddles and his deputy another.

The remaining seven riders turned their horses and rode for Sharon's store. Spurring his mount, Ethan rode down into the valley at a reckless gallop, determined to reach the store before anything could happen to Sharon. By the time he arrived the door was shut and locked and rifle barrels were pointing out of every window. Jackson knew that his dying wouldn't save Sharon and Corey, so he fought back the urge to rush the store with his gun blazing.

It was then that the door opened. Out stepped a white-haired man wearing a drooping moustache of the same color, with a face looking like it had been chiseled out of granite. The voice that came from him sounded like it was coming from the bottom of a well. "Are you Ethan Jackson?" he asked.

"I am," answered Ethan.

"I'm here for your brother, Cole."

"Figured you were," said Ethan. "What's your name?"

"Morgan Hawks."

"I've heard of you."

"Most folks have. Now, what about that brother of yours?"

"You have to take me on first."

"Figured on that."

"The street suit you?" asked Ethan.

"Reckon so," answered Hawks, who motioned with his left hand for Jackson to meet him in the middle of the street.

Walking in the direction that Hawks had indicated, Ethan stopped at fifty paces and faced Morgan. "One thing I'd like to ask you Hawks."

"Go ahead," said Morgan.

"I heard that Andy Adams was pretty much at death's door, so I'm wondering who paid you to kill my brother."

A grin seemed to crack across Hawks's face and he said, "Old man Adams ain't just standing at death's door anymore; he's opened it and walked on through."

"Then who's paying you for this?"

"He is. Or I suppose I ought to say he made arrangements to see I was paid when I bring proof to his lawyer that your brother is dead. You see, before he died he sold just about everything he owned, put it on Cole's head, and offered it to me to make sure your brother ends up dead."

Seeing that no amount of talking was going to stop Hawks from doing his job, Jackson flexed his fingers in preparation for his draw. He'd heard that Hawks was the fastest man with a gun who'd ever lived—bar none—and that he only pulled his gun when there was money involved. Remembering how rich Andy Adams had been, Jackson knew that Hawks had been given plenty of incentive to draw his weapon.

Settling into his stance, Morgan said, "I've been hearing that you've been trying to hang up your gun, Jackson, and get shut of your reputation as a gunfighter. Is that true?"

"Pretty much," answered Ethan.

Looking Jackson square in the eye, Hawks asked, "You figure that you still have a fast draw after staying out of gunfights for as long as you have?"

"Well, think of it like playing poker. You're going to have to pay to see my hand."

Morgan laughed, and then his hand swept back to make his draw. Ethan grabbed for his sidearm at the same time. While Ethan's speed was natural, Hawks's speed was not only natural, but honed to a fine edge through years of daily practice, which now paid off when his Colt came out of his holster a fraction of a second faster than Ethan's gun cleared his. It was what Morgan had expected, but he hadn't expected to feel the .45 slug ripping through his chest and severing his backbone.

Looking up from the dusty street where he had collapsed, he saw where Ethan was holding his gun. He'd fired from the hip; that had made up for his slower draw. "Damn," was the last word the professional gunman uttered.

Remembering that there were still six gunmen to deal with, Ethan ducked behind a building and reloaded his weapon. He didn't have to wait very long for the gunmen to make their move. They all came out of the store, using Sharon for a shield. Ethan looked for Corey and then remembered that he and Cole had planned to go fishing that day, so at least he wasn't in the line of fire. It was a good thing that he wasn't too, for several people in town had come out and were pointing weapons at the gunmen who were using Sharon as a shield.

Ethan dearly wanted Sharon out of his line of fire, for he knew that he couldn't let those men get to their horses where they would probably shoot her once they could run. It was then that Sharon decided to lend a helping hand by biting down on the arm of the man who was holding her out in front of him. The man screamed and quickly let go of his captor.

As soon as she was released she dropped to the ground and gunfire erupted from everywhere. Unfortunately for Ethan, the six killers looked upon him as the major threat and they all turned their guns on him instead of engaging any of the other people shooting at them.

Bullets were flying all around Ethan. One hit him in his right shoulder, another slashed his neck, yet another struck him in his right leg causing his knee to buckle. He dropped to the ground, still firing his revolver, until the hammer dropped on an empty chamber. All he could see was gun smoke for the few seconds before he passed out.

The doctor and concerned friends set up a vigil at Ethan's bedside for several days. His fate was still up in the air as to whether he would live or die. If he lived, there was a serious question as to whether he would still be a man capable of living the active life he had since he'd first learned to walk as a child, or whether he would finish his life as a cripple. And then there was his problematic reputation as a gunfighter, which had only increased with what had happened on the streets of Leantown. All of his work to shed himself of his fame along such lines was wasted now.

Luck still dogged his heels, and he recovered. On those rare occasions he found himself alone, he used the time to see if he could still use all his limbs. When the doctor told him that while he would be sore and stiff for quite some time, but that he would eventually be able to sling a gun again, he wasn't surprised. He was greatly disappointed, though, for he had hoped that he would be wounded just enough to give him an excuse to hang up his gun and live a peaceful life, far away from the reputation-hunting fools who plagued his very existence.

With such matters still on his mind, Ethan found it hard to fall asleep at night. Not wishing to add to this ailment, he refrained from asking anyone about what had happened to Baldwin and his deputy, for fear of hearing an answer he didn't want to know. His friends, having been warned by the doctor not to agitate him, refrained from telling him something he hadn't asked about.

Ethan also wasn't likely to get much information from the good doctor, who could never have been described as gabby. But when he was well enough to be propped up in front of the window that looked down on the town's main street, he could see pretty much everything that was going on in the community. He was pleased to see that all seemed once again to be running along smoothly. He took note that not one fight had broken out—even in the saloon. He even smiled when he saw children playing in the street that had only recently been the scene of a deadly gunfight. People he recognized were going about their business as if nothing had happened.

There was no getting around the fact that plenty had happened in Ethan's life, however, and as he began to get his strength back, he started to realize he couldn't hide from his problems. He was going to have to confront them sooner or later. So when Sharon and Jake made one of their frequent visits to his room, he worked up the nerve to ask the question that had been plaguing him for some time.

"How's Baldwin and his deputy?"

Looking quickly toward Jake to see if he thought she should answer the question, she saw him nod that she should. So she said, "The deputy died from his wounds, but the sheriff made it. The doctor says he should be back up and around about the same time as you."

Feeling relieved that his friend had survived, Ethan asked, "What about Hawks and his men?"

Jumping into the conversation, Jake announced, "That whole bunch is dead, in large part thanks to you. You see you nailed four of the last six, and the townspeople got the other two. And that don't even count Morgan Hawks. So when you count him, that means you got five of the ten hombres who rode in here."

Banging his balled fist against the chair arm, Ethan railed against fate as he said, "Well, that cuts it. I just outdrew Morgan Hawks and four of his men. Looks like I'm going to be cursed with the name of gunslinger until the day they throw dirt over me."

Jake smiled as he asked, "What about that wound to your shoulder? Won't it end your gunslingin'?"

Looking disgusted, Ethan said, "The doctor says I'll have full use of it once I heal up a mite."

"You must have been plumb groggy when you talked to the doc, for I just had a long conversation with the sawbones and after I told him what your situation was and all, he just plumb up and said that your wounded shoulder would cause you to be permanently disabled and that your days of slinging a gun were over for good."

As the importance of what his friend had said began to dawn on him, Jackson looked across at Sharon, who had tears welling up in her eyes. She reached over and squeezed his hand, smiling.